COME A LITTLE CLOSER

MEN OF THE MISFIT INN BOOK 4

KAIT NOLAN

Do you need more small town sass and spark? Sign up for <u>my newsletter</u> to hear about new releases, book deals, and exclusive content!

Want to get social? Join me in <u>Kait's Cantina!</u>

A LETTER TO READERS

Dear Reader,

Before I get to my usual warning, I want to ask if you knew that this isn't where Sam and Griff's story starts? They have a prequel novella, *Until We Meet Again,* that tells their backstory. It's set eight years before this book. You can read the novel without it, but by then end I promise you'll want to go back, so why not start there?

This book features characters from the Deep South. As such, it contains a great deal of colorful, colloquial, and occasionally grammatically incorrect language. This is a deliberate choice on my part as an author to most accurately represent the region where I have lived my entire life. This book also contains swearing and pre-marital sex between the lead couple, as those things are part of the realistic lives of characters of this generation, and of many of my readers.

If any of these things are not your cup of tea, please consider that you may not be the right audience for this book. There are scores of other books out there that are written with you in mind. In fact, I've got a list of some of my favorite authors who write on the sweeter side on my website at https://kaitnolan.com/on-the-sweeter-side/

If you choose to stick with me, I hope you enjoy!

Happy reading!

Kait

CHAPTER 1

"Why did I agree to this wedding?" Samantha Ferguson scowled at the familiar stretch of tree-lined mountain road she could drive in her sleep. "I hate weddings."

From the car speakers, Audrey Graham's voice was dry. "I hope you don't, since you agreed to be in mine."

She'd done so without a qualm, delighted that one of her best friends had found love with an amazing man. Watching the two of them fall for each other at a grown-up summer camp last year had been an absolute joy, even if it had given her a bit of a pinch around her own heart.

"You and Hudson aren't the same."

"And why is that?"

"For one, I'm not going to know the entire wedding party, and the entire wedding party is not going to have a whole boatload of stories about me that I'd rather forget. With Erin, there's this whole getting-the-band-back-together vibe. I haven't seen a lot of these people at all since high school and college, and we weren't exactly all buddy-buddy to begin with. It was one of those situations where she and I were friends, and I was tangentially associated with the rest of them."

How often had that been the case over the years? Her circles had always been small, which never bothered her until ceremony and celebration called for her to play nice with others. There was nothing like being thrust into a larger group to make her feel like an outsider.

"Is it really the whole idea of having to deal with people from high school that has you in a dither? You're not normally this agitated about the idea of going home."

Sam blew out a breath, unable to muster any annoyance at her friend for putting on her therapist's hat. "I hated high school. You know that. It wasn't me. I didn't fit in, and I spent so much time and effort working to get myself away from all of that. I'm afraid that coming back for this wedding party bonding weekend crap is just gonna involve a whole lot of me getting forced back into roles that I don't want to remember." Just the idea of it had her shoulders bunching and her hands tightening on the steering wheel.

"Can they really force you back without your permission?"

With a fresh scowl, Sam took the turn onto Main Street, automatically slowing as she rolled into what constituted downtown Eden's Ridge. "I think I liked it better when you weren't pursuing the shrinky side of your training, Dr. Graham. It's not so simple as permission. Obviously, there's a conscious element to all this. But the bride and groom were a thing in high school, and I'm pretty sure they have much fonder memories of that experience than I do, and are probably going to be playing that up, now that they've found each other again. Oh, and then there's the fact that my high school nemesis is the matron of honor."

"You had a high school nemesis?" Audrey's tone piqued with interest, and Sam knew she was turning the idea of it over in her head. A certified prodigy, Audrey had graduated at fifteen, so she hadn't had most of the normal high school experiences.

"Cressida Gilcrest. Well, Milton now. She was a total Regina George. Except she never actually got her comeuppance and never became a better human. She's Erin's cousin, which is the only reason she's a part of this. Family pressure."

"Uh huh. And facing her down means what, exactly?"

"Having my always-a-bridesmaid status thrown in my face." *Among other things.*

"What does that matter? You've never de-fined yourself by your relationship status."

Sam's back twitched, the tattoo on her shoulder seeming to burn. It and the memories it evoked were old, but the wound still throbbed. That was the real reason this weekend had her out of sorts. But she didn't confess that truth to Audrey. She'd never con-fessed it to anyone.

"You're right. Of course, you're right."

"I usually am."

"Har har."

Audrey laughed. "It's three days. You can handle it. There are worse things in the world than spending a long weekend at a spa."

"If this was all massages, facials, and pedi-cures, I'd be a lot less anxious about it." Seeing an open parking spot along the curb a block down from her mom's shop, Sam whipped into it.

"Well, put on your big girl panties because there's nothing to do about it but get through it.

Didn't you tell me your bestie from high school was a bridesmaid, too?"

At the reminder, Sam's mind turned away from the hurt. "She is, thank God. Jill's been in Atlanta for many years now, trying to get a music career off the ground while working other jobs to pay the bills, and I've been on the publish or perish train, so it's been ages since we've actually connected. She's the lone silver lining of the weekend. We'll be able to bemoan our mutual single status together among all the marrieds."

"There you go. Focus on that and forget the rest."

"Right." The long exhale only released a little of the tension. She needed a change of subject before her too-observant friend started digging into more of the whys behind this anxiety. "In other news, how is my brother? I mean, I know you can't give me specifics because of the whole doctor-patient confidentiality thing, but generally how is he doing? He's been all incommunicado since he got up to Syracuse to start your program."

"He's good. He baked a chocolate tart this week that almost made me weep."

"I can't get over the fact that you're teaching my brother to be a baker." After more than a decade as a Navy SEAL, Jonah was finally out and working through his transition to civilian life in Audrey's experimental treatment program.

"Well, let's be accurate. My future husband's cousin, Rachel, is the one who's doing the teaching. Overall, the program is performing well above my expectations. Who would have thought that this would be an excellent treatment modality for PTSD, depression, and anxiety in a bunch of hardcore former military guys?"

"You did. And that's why you're the certified genius."

"Fair point. Now quit procrastinating and go get this over with. You'll feel better when it's done."

Busted. "Okay, okay, I know you're right, I'm gonna go. Do me a favor and tell Jonah to call home. I want to hear his voice and check in with him. Mom will definitely want the same."

"I'll let him know. Now, I want you to remember that I'm a professional, so hear me when I say this: You are a badass, intelligent, beautiful adult woman. Whatever shades of high school rear their ugly heads this weekend, you are not that person anymore, and nobody can make you be. Talk to you on the other side. I love you, girl."

Though Audrey couldn't see, Sam smiled. "Yeah, I love you, too."

Hanging up the phone, she slid out of the car and into the cool October weather. Happy-faced pansies in concrete planters bobbed in the breeze as she made the short trek down the street to the salon known locally by all and sundry as the Snort 'n Curl, so dubbed because her mother, a former Miss Tennessee finalist, believed in big hair and big laughs. Her clients could count on both. That big, bawdy laugh rolled out the moment Sam tugged open the door, along with the chatter of cheerful female conversation.

The familiar scents of shampoo and the vaguely chemical undertone of hair dye and bleach drew her inside, back into her childhood. So much of her time growing up had been spent helping out in the shop, shampooing, sweeping up, doing homework. Snared in the past, she didn't immediately speak up. Here was comfort, camaraderie. Here was home, as much as the little three-bedroom she'd once shared just a mile-and-a-half up the road.

From beneath one of the bonnet dryers, Jolene Lowrey looked up. "Why, Samantha!"

Conversation came to a stop like the screech of a record.

Sam worked up a polite smile. "Mrs. Lowrey. Good to see you."

Rebecca set her comb and shears aside and rushed over, arms open wide. "Hey, baby girl!"

As those arms closed around her, another few layers of tension dropped away. "Hey,

Mama." Sam burrowed in, briefly resting her head against her mother's shoulder as she wrestled with the guilt of not coming home as often as she should.

"It's so good to see you." Rebecca pulled back, looked her over with assessing eyes the same shape as Sam's. "You look a mite tired, honey."

Sam's lips twitched. "Good thing I'm here for a spa weekend, then."

"Girls' trip?"

She glanced over at the woman in the chair for a cut, recognizing Essie Vaughn, the dispatcher and admin for the Sheriff's Department. "Not exactly. I'm in town for a bachelor/bachelorette party bonding sort of deal for Erin Ashby and Kendrick Teague. Their wedding's coming up in a couple months, so they're getting everybody together at The Misfit Inn and Spa for the weekend."

From the chair at the other station, Patty Hodgson tapped her lips. "Why do I remember his name?"

"He was star quarterback when I was in high school," Sam supplied.

"Oh yes, remember?" Essie prompted. "He got scouted by UT. Went pro for a few years."

Rebecca returned to her station and resumed combing out and cutting Essie's hair. "Married some girl from out in California, I thought."

Essie nodded. "He did. She divorced him when he blew out his knee and lost his career."

"What about the Ashby girl?" Candice French continued to place rollers in Patty's hair. "I thought she married Galen Banks."

With an expression that was part pity, part superiority that she wasn't as out of the loop as her stylist, Patty closed the magazine on her lap and crossed her legs. "She did. Moved off to Memphis, I think. They got divorced, too."

Amused at the play-by-play, Sam couldn't help clarifying. "They were high school sweethearts. Both of them came back to the Ridge to work at the high school. They reconnected and fell back in love. It's pretty adorable, really."

Even from her jaded perspective, she had to admit that. Love did come back around for some people.

"So lovely that they found their way back to each other." Essie sighed with the kind of contentment she'd often been known to display after finishing a good romance novel. Perking up, her eyes flicked to Sam's in the mirror. "What about you, dear? When are you going to walk down the aisle? Is there anybody special?"

The question was uttered in a cheerfully nosy tone that had Sam struggling not to grit her teeth. Because there wasn't anyone special. There hadn't been in more years than she cared to admit, and that trod far too close to the real reason weddings made her bitter. Because everyone pitied her for her perpetually single status, and no one knew she'd married and divorced at twenty-two. Then again, a marriage that lasted hardly longer than it took for the ink to dry didn't really count, did it?

Usually, she managed to shove that negativity down. But Kendrick had been a close friend and foster brother to Griff, and she didn't want all those memories stirred back up. At least her ex-husband was still in the Marines, still off God knew where, doing God knew what. She hoped he was safe, then cursed herself. Griffin Powell was no longer hers to worry about. He'd made his choice years ago, and it hadn't been her.

With no intention of sharing one of the most painful parts of her past, Sam forced another smile and focused on her mother. "I just spoke to Audrey on the way here. She said Jonah's doing well and promised to make sure he calls home."

Rebecca nodded in satisfaction. "Oh good. I've been sending care packages, but the boy hasn't done more than send a few emails since he got up there."

"Where is he these days?" Patty asked.

"Upstate New York, in a program to help him transition from the SEALs to civilian life. He's training to be a master baker," Rebecca explained.

As conversation turned to the safer topic of her brother, Sam backed toward the door. "I need to be getting on. They're expecting me up at the inn. I just wanted to stop in and say hello."

"You're sure you won't stay at the house?" Rebecca asked.

"That would defeat the purpose of all of Erin's planned bonding activities. But I promise to stop by again before I head out. Love you, Mama."

"Love you, too, baby."

Check-in and farewells completed, she made a hasty exit, wishing the rest of the weekend would pass as quickly.

GRIFFIN POWELL WAS a man who understood duty. Twelve years in the Marines had seen to that. He made only those promises he believed he could keep, and he'd promised Kendrick he'd be here for this bizarre excuse for a bachelor party, even though he'd rather run fifteen miles uphill with a hundred pounds of gear strapped to his back. Because Kendrick was his brother, and that's what brothers did. It wasn't Kendrick's fault that coming home felt so complicated, or that weddings in general left Griff feeling edgy and restless.

No, that was entirely his own fault because of promises made and broken to a woman he'd never gotten out of his mind. A woman it was past time he sought out again. Griff was man enough to admit he was afraid of the reception he'd get. Afraid, too, of finding out she'd moved on with her life, as he'd freed her to do so many years ago. It had been the right thing for them both. He'd clung to that. Had to, or he'd never have been able to walk away. But that didn't mean he hadn't bled. Samantha had been his greatest love, and he wasn't ready to give up hope that he could still win her back.

Maybe he'd use this weekend to do a little digging. Find out where she was. If anyone knew whether she'd married. The idea tied his gut in knots. She and Erin had been friends once. Surely someone knew. With all the inevitable walking down memory lane, Sam would probably get mentioned without him having to say a word. He'd just have to bide his time and listen. He'd gotten good at that.

As he pulled up to the three-story Victorian that had been his home for the last three years of high school, Griff was grateful it wasn't his first trip back. The awkward had already been broached with his sisters earlier this year when he'd come as bodyguard to Kyle Keenan, and Kyle had been the prodigal in that scenario. Another foster brother, Kyle had become a rampant success as a country music star and finally come home to fix things with the woman who'd been his childhood best friend turned enemy. As Abbey was now his wife and they were expecting their first child, that had all turned out all right in the end. Griff could only pray for such an outcome for himself.

Shaking off the somber mood, he dug up a smile and jogged up the steps, slipping through the front door. It still felt right and comfortable to do that, though the home where he'd grown up had been turned into an inn. A part of him still expected his foster mother, Joan Reynolds, to come out of the kitchen, arms open wide for a hug. She'd been gone more than three years now, but he still felt the pang at her loss. At least until his sister, Kennedy, stepped out of the kitchen herself.

"Well, well. Look what the cat dragged in." Despite her tone, she was all smiles as she crossed the foyer, wrapping him in a warm hug of her own. "Welcome, home."

Griff squeezed her back. "Hey, sis. How are Xander and the baby?"

"He's protecting and serving and happy as a clam. The man was born to be Sheriff. And Caroline is growing like a weed. She's started walking now and is into every blessed thing." Kennedy's grin communicated her absolute delight with her daughter. "How was the drive?"

"Eh, fine. No problems. Anybody here yet?"

"Oh yeah, everybody's been arriving all afternoon." She raised her voice. "Kendrick! Your brother's here."

The groom himself poked his head out of the living room that was now technically the guest lounge. A blinding white smile flashed in his dark face as he bulleted across the room, catching Griff around the middle in a move that was as much tackle as hug because they'd once been teammates as well as brothers. Griff set his stance, absorbed the momentum, and hauled Kendrick into a rib-cracking hug himself. After a series of grunts and back thumps, they pulled back to beam at each other.

"Damn, it's good to see you, brother!" Kendrick's gaze swept the foyer. "Where's Mateo? I thought he was riding up with you from Nashville."

"He sends his regrets." Griff rocked back on his heels and shoved his hands into his back pockets. "He's not gonna be able to make it this weekend. His office manager recently quit, so there's nobody to manage the gym while he's away. But he promises he'll be here with bells on for the wedding."

"Damn. We'll miss him. But we're glad you made it." Erin Ashby, Kendrick's clearly besotted bride-to-be, crossed over to offer her own hug. "It's good to see you again."

"You, too." Out of long ingrained habit, he gave a gentle tug on Erin's blonde ponytail, making her laugh. "Who else is here?"

"Declan got in last night," Kendrick explained, mentioning yet another of their brothers. "Mick's working up at Thompson's Garage these days. He'll be along after work. And Erin's brother, Ryder—you remember him? He was a few years ahead of us. Married Lewis Washington a few years back. They run Forbidden Fruit Cidery now. He'll be by tonight with plenty of cider for the bonfire."

"About half my bridesmaids are here." Erin snuggled up against Kendrick's side. "Roxanne and Mariko."

"Did we hear our names?" A polished black woman in a neat pantsuit stepped out of the lounge, trailed by a petite Asian woman with laughing brown eyes and a waterfall of ebony hair.

"Ladies." Griff nodded in acknowledgement.

"And Cressida is here as well." Erin didn't quite manage to hide her speculative look. "She's in the spa at the moment."

Griff held in his wince. Barely. He hadn't seen his high-school girlfriend in more years than he cared to count, and he wasn't eager to break the streak. She was just one of a long line of bad decisions from back then, none of which he wanted to remember.

Kendrick smirked. "She's married now."

"Thank God."

Erin's peal of laughter echoed in the foyer. "Good to know your taste has improved with age."

He offered a noncommittal grunt. He hadn't actually liked Cressida much when he'd dated her. She hadn't mattered, and that had been the whole point. She'd been convenient, and they'd used each other for their own ends. Not something he was proud of, but so little of his life back then could be looked at without cringing.

By his count, there were still a couple more bridesmaids unaccounted for. Griff realized he didn't have any idea who the rest of the bridal party was. He'd just agreed to be a groomsman for Kendrick without asking questions, trusting the rest would take care of itself. Before he could inquire about who else Erin had asked to stand up with her on her big day, the front door opened behind him. Griff turned in time to catch the bump of a rolling suitcase as a woman stepped into the room.

Everything inside him went still, and time seemed to slow and stretch as she straightened.

He wasn't prepared for this. Hadn't expected to see her. Not here. Not yet.

She was as beautiful as ever. Older, a little more polished, but she still bore the same faint smattering of freckles across her cheeks that looked like stars, still wore her mass of glossy brown hair long and loose. His fingers itched to reach out and touch her. To reacquaint himself with the silky feel of her hair, her skin. With the remembered taste of her mouth.

He'd taken half a step in her direction before she looked up, and he met those eyes that had haunted his dreams.

CHAPTER 2

*S*am stepped through the front door of the inn, already registering the babble of voices, and wondered if it was too late to book a massage at the spa. She hauled her suitcase over the threshold and looked up, right into the sea-blue eyes of the biggest mistake of her life. The sucker punch of it had her mouth falling open, her breath escaping in a silent gust. If she'd had anything in her hands, it would have fallen from nerveless fingers.

Griffin Powell. Former high school running

back. Bad boy. Tutee. And, for a blink eight years ago, her husband.

He was here, in the flesh. Safe. Whole. Relief was another mule kick to her chest. But it was the stunning shock that he'd really come back for her that nearly took her to her knees. Then the fury boiled up, fresh and bright, straightening her spine and the limbs that wanted to shake.

"Oh my God, Sam! I'm so glad you made it!"

Hugs. Someone was hugging her. Erin. Breaking her paralysis, Sam wrapped her arms mechanically around the bride, using the gesture to cover her reaction. Some distant part of her mind managed conversation, saying all the right social things while she managed a surreptitious glance at Griff. For all the years she'd known him, he'd always been incredibly self-possessed. She'd never guessed at his feelings for her in high school. But he didn't quite hide his shock at seeing her now.

So he hadn't come back for her. The knowledge was a fresh slash across her heart, and she called herself a fool for believing he would, even for a moment. She knew better.

He was here for Kendrick, likely part of the wedding party, same as she was. She managed to avoid him as she ran the gauntlet, sharing slightly awkward hugs with Roxanne and Mariko and more real ones with Declan Callahan and Kendrick himself. And then she was out of people, no longer able to avoid confronting her big, ginger mistake.

Griff spoke first. "Samantha."

She curled her toes, fighting the shudder at hearing her full name on his lips. His voice was rougher, gruffer than she remembered. It was all too easy to imagine it growling in her ear as he gave her unspeakable pleasure. Every cell in her body wanted to lean toward him, to erase the distance of years and miles. She held firm, angling her head and keeping her tone dialed to the vague interest she showed recalcitrant students who spun wild excuses for why they hadn't turned in assignments on time.

"Griffin."

His eyes darkened, and too late she remembered that he'd loved her prim teacher's voice.

Oblivious to the tension, Erin grinned. "Oh, of course. I forgot you two knew each other from tutoring."

Right. Tutoring. And a weekend in Vegas a lifetime ago. Sam nodded at him, not really trusting herself to speak.

Kendrick waded in. "We were damned lucky this guy's finally out of the Marines now, and off the tour with Kyle, so he could be here." He slapped Griff on the shoulder, not catching the faint wince.

But she did.

So he'd evidently been out of the service for a while now. And hadn't sought her out as he'd claimed he would all those years ago. It was what she'd expected, so why should the truth of it hurt?

Griff opened his mouth, as if he wanted to say something, but Sam shifted her attention to Erin. "Is Jill here yet?"

"Not yet. She's our last holdout. But hopefully she'll get here before the festivities tonight."

Please God. "What are we doing?"

Erin linked a companionable arm through Sam's "Having a good old-fashioned bonfire. Only with legal drinking this time."

Sam remembered the bonfires from high school. The drunk. The stupid. The rowdy. She'd avoided them most of the time. But she fixed a smile on her face. "Great."

Sensing rather than seeing Griff take a step toward her, she turned to Kennedy. "I'd really like to get checked in and settled."

"No problem."

After sorting the paperwork, Kennedy's teenaged niece, Ari, led her up to a corner room on the second floor. She was a cheerful, engaging kid, who obviously enjoyed people.

"Bathroom's down the hall. Do you have a plus one on the way?"

Sam's shoulders tensed, but she bit back the instinctive defensiveness. There wasn't a malicious tone to the question. "Why?"

"Just making sure you don't need extra towels."

"Ah. No. Just me. Thanks."

"If you need anything, just let me know."

As the girl turned to go, Sam called out. "Do you happen to know who else is on this floor?"

"Oh, Roxanne and Mariko. And Cressida."

Sam couldn't stop the cringe.

Ari laughed. "Yeah, I kinda thought she was one of those. She's at the far end. Griff's across the hall. Everybody else is on the third floor."

"Thanks." Across the freaking hall. Was she going to have to worry about running into him on the way to the bathroom in the middle of the night?

With a cheery wave, Ari left her alone.

Sam shut the door and sank down on the bed, letting the reaction come. Her body shook and her eyes burned, but she refused to let the tears fall. She'd shed enough over him. But Christ. He was here. A part of her had believed she'd never see him again. The hard-shelled, self-protective part had hoped she wouldn't because just the sight of him had ripped open the scars on her heart.

She didn't want this. Didn't want to feel. To remember. To want.

He wasn't for her. He'd made that clear.

And now she was going to be stuck hanging around him for the next three days? And again for the wedding next month?

Flopping back onto the bed, she rolled to bury her face in a pillow to muffle a short scream.

She needed distraction. She needed backup. She needed Jill.

So thinking, she dug out her phone and dialed.

Voicemail picked up at once. "This is Jill. You know what to do."

"Girl, I hope you're almost here because I don't know how I'm going to get through this weekend without you. I can't wait to see you."

Hanging up, she tossed the phone aside and wondered how long she could hide.

* * *

THE BONFIRE SNAPPED AND CRACKLED, sending sparks up into the velvet black sky and radiating heat out against the chill. From his position between his brothers, Griff watched the group and listened. Ryder's spectacular cider had flowed freely, and they could credit their sister Athena's chili for the fact that nobody was truly drunk yet—though most of the wedding party was making a valiant effort to get there. It wasn't so different from high school, with the giggling and preening of the girls and the posturing from the guys.

Still nursing his second cider, Griff held back, uncomfortable with the dynamic of nostalgia and the inevitable discussion of the glory days. High school hadn't been that for him. He'd been a delinquent as much as an athlete, and he wasn't that guy anymore. A huge part of the reason for that was the woman sitting as far as she could get from him.

"Man, I haven't done this in forever." With a

bemused grin, Declan tipped his cider back. "Feels good to pretend to be something other than the grown-up, who has to have it all figured out."

"Oh, are we supposed to know that by now? My bad. I'm falling behind." Kendrick clinked his bottle to Declan's. "Least I finally got the woman right."

Erin blew him a kiss.

"Better late than never," Declan agreed. "I sure as hell haven't had luck on that front. Not that I've been looking since I got full custody of Scarlett. Taking care of her is taking all the bandwidth I've got."

"You wouldn't change a thing, though, would you?" Erin asked.

Declan hesitated. "I wouldn't wish my daughter away, no. But there was a conversation with someone I wish I'd had back when, before I left."

"Oh ho! I smell a juicy story." Ryder held out a fresh cider. "Spill it."

Eying the bottle, Declan shrugged and accepted it. "Why the hell not? I'm not driving, and Scarlett's with Ari." He settled back, twisted off the cap.

"So what did you wish you'd said to Scarlett's mother?" Roxanne prompted.

Declan blinked. "Nothing. We said everything we needed to say through lawyers. I was talking about someone else. After Scarlett's mom and I split, but before I knew she was pregnant."

"Oh, yeah." Ryder angled his head, obviously thinking back. "That was the summer we were all working out at the orchard, right? You had a little thing going with Abbey's cousin, didn't you? What was her name? Liza? Lena?"

"Livia." Just her name put a far-off look in Declan's eyes, a soft tone in his voice.

Griff could relate. It took everything he had not to stare over at Sam, who was, as she'd always been, the observer. She'd rarely come to bonfires back then, and had been as likely as not to stay camped out in a car with a book and a flashlight, rather than participating in what could loosely have been termed socializing. She'd have talked if Jill were here, but the last bridesmaid still hadn't arrived. So she sat a little apart, occasionally contributing to the conversation, otherwise reading on her phone.

"So what was the story with her?" Mariko asked.

"There's not much of one. Nothing happened between us. Not past some really spectacular kisses."

"But you wanted it to," Ryder prompted.

"Oh, hell yes, I did."

"What ever happened to her?" Kendrick asked.

"Don't know. I found out about Scarlett, and I never saw her again."

"Dude, that's just sad," Mick declared. "Why didn't you get her number from Abbey?"

"So I could say what? 'Hey, sorry I bailed on you. I just found out I'm a father?' Yeah, that was gonna go over super well when we were eighteen."

"It's never too late for an apology."

Sam's statement was quiet, and she was most definitely not looking in his direction, but Griff understood the message was for him as well. Or maybe that was just wishful thinking—the idea that an apology could fix what he'd broken. The effort she'd put into avoiding him made it perfectly clear that she wouldn't just fall back into his arms. Not that he'd expected it to be that easy. The best things never were.

"It's been years. I doubt she even remembers me."

"Oh, don't sell yourself short, honey. We all have fond memories of our high school sweethearts." Cressida shot a none-too-subtle smile in Griff's direction before glancing with pity at Sam. "Well, some of us."

Sam didn't rise to the bait, keeping her focus on Declan instead. "What is it you wish you'd said to her?"

"I don't know exactly. Given where my life went, it wasn't as if we could've been anything. Just... I wish I'd at least said a proper goodbye."

He jerked his shoulders again. "Not like I can say that now."

She blinked those deep, dark eyes, gaze shifting to the fire. "Closure is worth a hell of a lot. Maybe she's thought of you all these years. Maybe she hasn't. But that open loop obviously bothers you, so what's the harm in getting her number from Abbey and telling her what you need to?"

"I guess it's fear. That I hurt her worse than I meant to. Or possibly that our time together meant more to me than it did to her." Declan frowned. "That might be worse."

Wasn't that the damned truth? Griff wanted an open, honest conversation with Sam, not all this cross-speak and subtext. But it was what he had for the moment, so he added his two cents. "The right woman is worth facing the fear."

Declan's brows drew together. "How the hell did we all decide that my end-of-high-school summer fling was the right woman? I'm just getting my nostalgia on."

Mariko shot him a speculative look. "Some

women really dig single dads." At his bland stare, she lifted her cider. "I'm just saying. Seeing Clayton with his son was an absolute game-changer for me. Here was this guy who had his shit together, had the emotional maturity to take excellent care of his child without getting all mired in toxic masculinity or socially expected gender roles. I totally fell in love with them both."

"Be that as it may, I'm already considering major changes for Scarlett and me. I don't want to shake up her world by adding a woman to the mix."

"What changes?" Erin wanted to know.

"We need to get out of Nashville. I'm thinking of moving back to the Ridge. I want home and family."

Kendrick wrapped him in a back-thumping hug. "That's awesome, man! We'd love to have you back. And everybody's been enjoying the hell out of your girl. She's a pistol."

"She'll be more of one if she keeps hanging out with Ari, but I kind of love the idea of that,"

Declan admitted. "I can't give her siblings, but I can give her cousins aplenty. I think that'd be good for her."

"Joan made sure we could all appreciate that." As his heart pinched, Griff raised his bottle. "To family. The ones we chose and the ones who chose us."

The toast echoed around the fire.

As conversation shifted once more, Griff risked a look at Sam. She hadn't moved, but still seemed to have pulled back in on herself. Something in her posture set her apart from the group, though she sat in the huddle like everyone else, perched on one of the folding camp chairs. She didn't want to be here. He understood that and wondered if it was purely because of him or if there was something else. Even as he watched her, she lifted her phone again.

"Girl, are you surgically attached to that phone?" Roxanne asked. "Can't you spend a single weekend away from your man?"

Griff tensed. Her man. Had she moved on, after all?

"Whoever she's texting, it's not a man. She's single." Cressida made the pronouncement in an unmistakable bless-her-heart tone.

Even as the insult was delivered, he sent up a prayer of thanks that he wasn't too late.

Erin rolled her eyes. "Must you be so insufferable? The world does not revolve around people's relationship status. Women *do* have value without a man."

"I never said they didn't."

Sam didn't quite hide the flash of temper. Griff could imagine the comebacks scrolling through that big brain of hers, none of which she actually let fly.

"I was just trying to reach Jill again. Has anybody heard from her?"

"Oh, she's probably bailing. She's always been a flake," Cressida announced.

A muscle jumped in Sam's jaw, but her tone remained mild. "It's not like her not to notify someone if she can't make it somewhere. She should have been here by now."

Erin squeezed her shoulder. "I'm sure Jill's fine. She asked earlier this week whether festivities were starting tonight or in the morning, so I think there was something she was having to juggle to be here."

The noncommittal noise made it clear Sam wasn't satisfied with that explanation, but she slid the phone back into her pocket.

Mariko leapt into the awkward silence. "We should play some sort of game."

"A drinking game," Mick added. "This cider is too damned good for anything else."

"Why thank you, my good man." Ryder clinked his bottle to Mick's.

"I know!" Erin crowed. "Let's play Never Have I Ever!"

CHAPTER 3

Oh, for the love of God.

Sam wanted to escape. Wanted to walk away from all this idiocy and get some space, find some peace. But she'd promised Erin she'd be here, and that meant participating in whatever lunacy the happy couple came up with. Of course, she'd expected Jill to be by her side, and she hadn't known Griff would be here.

She'd assumed he was still deployed... somewhere. Her standard operating procedure for years had been trying *not* to think about where he was or what he was doing, something she'd had plenty of experience with because of her Navy SEAL brother. Now all her considerable will was going toward pretending Griff wasn't sitting on the other side of the fire. How the hell could he be more sexy and magnetic now than he was at twenty-two? Was it the beard? The dark red shadow of it highlighted that strong jaw. Her fingers itched to touch, to trace, to remember.

And that way lay madness.

Ryder supplied everyone with fresh cider. She considered overindulging. An alcoholic haze might drown out this tangle of lust and hurt and relief and that tender thing she refused to examine too closely. But it might also loosen her tongue or, worse, make her forget all the reasons she wasn't dragging her ex-husband behind the nearest door to give him a piece of her mind—and then her body.

Christ, nobody had ever stirred her like he did. Even with all the years of pain and anger, she still wanted him. Every moment of that long-ago night was as indelibly etched into her brain as the words in her skin.

And so was the morning after.

Better to keep her wits about her. This was the last group she felt safe airing her dirty laundry to. Still, a second cider after this many hours wouldn't hurt. She'd endure the game until she could come up with a reasonable excuse to head up to her room. If the headache that had been clawing through her system kept ratcheting up, she'd have true reason enough.

"Okay, it was my idea. I'll start." Erin screwed up her face. "Never have I ever lied to get out of going to work."

Everyone lifted their bottles.

Ryder grinned. "Me next. Never have I ever stood someone up on a date."

Sam, Mariko, and Kendrick were the only ones who didn't drink. Sam considered a date or two she wished she'd bailed on, but in the end hadn't been able to do it.

Mick waggled his brows. "Never have I ever gone skinny dipping."

Sam stayed still, finger tapping against the bottle as everybody else drank. When her turn rolled around, she sighed. "Never have I ever cheated on a test or exam."

This time it was she and Roxanne sitting it out.

"Well, that's the world's biggest non-surprise," Cressida snarked.

Play continued, revealing, as she'd known it would, exactly how poorly she fit in with this crowd.

"Never have I ever trespassed." Again, she sat out while everyone else drank and cheered.

Kendrick took his turn, tugging Erin to him. "Never have I ever loved anyone more than this woman."

"Aww, babe." She melted into him, taking a long, lingering kiss after he had his drink.

Griff's gaze swept the group. "Never have I ever gotten a tattoo I regretted."

Sam's fingers tensed on the bottle. His attention didn't linger on her, but she understood the question was for her. Did she regret her tattoo? Griff had the other half of the quote inked over the heart he'd once claimed she'd captured. It had been part of that whirlwind romance in Vegas, a means of immortalizing the trip in her memory. It had lasted where their marriage had not.

Before she'd decided, the game had moved on, taking a decidedly naughty turn.

"Never have I ever sent a sexy selfie."

"Never have I ever been to an adult store."

"Never have I ever faked an orgasm."

"Never have I ever flashed someone."

Question after question, others drank while she stayed put, feeling more and more out of place. The conservative academic didn't belong here. She never had.

Mick's voice was a little slurred as he stated, "Never have I ever gotten married in Vegas."

Sam's chest went tight. She could sit here, exactly as she had for the last dozen questions, not moving. No one here expected her to have done something as crazy as getting married in Vegas. But a part of her wanted to surprise them, wanted to prove she wasn't the girl she'd been in high school. Griff's gaze was a physical weight as she lifted her bottle, and she couldn't help watching to see if he'd drink, too. They were the only ones who did.

"No way!" Ryder exclaimed.

"Holy shit! Really, Sam?" Erin bounced in Kendrick's lap.

She shrugged. "It was a long time ago. Something impulsive I did at the start of grad school."

Roxanne leaned forward, clearly invested. "What happened?"

Sam wasn't about to give any details. This crowd needed no further reason to pity her. "Like so many things, it stayed in Vegas."

"What about you, bro?" Kendrick wanted to know.

"It was a trip I took between my two stints in the Marines."

Because everyone was looking at Griff, Sam let herself drink him in, the broad, muscular sweep of shoulders, the glint of fire in his deep red hair. As the rest of the group peppered him with questions, he didn't look at her, didn't do a thing to give it away. Of course, it never occurred to any of them that they'd married each other. Because, of course, it wouldn't. He'd been the bad boy jock. She'd only been his brainiac tutor.

Maybe that was all she'd ever been.

At the end of her tolerance, Sam rose. "I've had a long day. I think I'm going to turn in."

Erin was the only one who protested. "Aw, are you sure?"

Sam worked up a smile. "Yeah. Y'all have fun turning into pumpkins."

"'K. Sleep well. Don't be late to breakfast in the morning. We've got special activities planned."

"I'll be there with bells on."

A smattering of goodnights followed her as she made her way toward the house.

The tight band around her chest loosened with every step away from the group.

One night down. Two days to go.

Relieved to be free, she stopped on the wrap-around porch and checked her phone again. Still nothing from Jill. Knowing it was possibly overkill, she sent another text and tried calling again. Straight to voicemail. Well, Erin had said Jill had been juggling something. Maybe her band had landed a big gig tonight? It didn't explain why she hadn't let anyone know, but it would account for why she hadn't answered any texts or calls.

"You okay?"

At the quiet rumble of Griff's voice, Sam went rigid. How had she not heard him come after her? She'd been dreading this moment, doing everything she could to avoid it from the second she'd seen him in the foyer. Because what the hell would he say to her? What could he say that would make up for what he'd done?

Clinging tight to her phone, she squared her shoulders and turned to face him. "Why wouldn't I be?"

"Cressida is still a grade-A bitch, and you're still her favorite target. Add to that, the muscle in your left temple's been jumping for at least an hour." He lifted a hand, as if to touch her, but dropped it when she took an instinctive step back. "That headache's bound to be a whopper."

She hated that he'd noticed that. Hated that he could still read her. The pain had dug its talons in on top of her skull, squeezing, squeezing until she felt the pain behind her eyes. She'd mostly been able to ignore it until now. But she was tired, so tired of keeping up appearances, of holding back the tide of every-thing she felt, and that only made her head throb worse. "What do you want, Griff?"

"To talk."

She couldn't stop the bitter huff of laughter. "Talk. Because you're suddenly big on that."

He paused, seeming to consider his words as he glanced back to make sure the others were still at the fire. "We made, as you said, an impul-sive decision in Vegas eight years ago."

"One you regretted. I don't see what we have to talk about."

"I didn't regret it."

It was the urgency in his tone that had her turning toward him. "What?"

"I didn't regret marrying you. Didn't you get my letter?" He took a step closer, and she took yet another in retreat, finding her escape route blocked by a chaise lounge.

"Yeah, I found it." Along with legal documents dissolving their newly minted hopes and dreams.

He said nothing, but she could feel the weight of his gaze in the dark, waiting for some kind of reaction.

His words had made her bleed, tearing out the foolishly romantic heart that had carried her through that crazy weekend and leaving bitterness and empty promises behind. She'd wept far too many tears over this man, and damn if she didn't feel more welling up inside her, pressing against that wavering control. She didn't intend to give him more.

Needing a barrier between them, she folded her arms. "You didn't know I'd be here any more than I was expecting you. That was plain enough. You do not seriously expect me to believe you're coming back for me after all these years."

"In a formally planned effort this weekend, no. But that doesn't change the fact that I meant what I said, Samantha."

She'd meant what she said, too. Meant the vows that she'd made. He hadn't. It infuriated her that just seeing him again had the pain of that betrayal bleeding fresh. Riding on the wave of it, she stepped toward him, keeping her voice low as much to hide the threat of tears as to keep the others from overhearing. "You left me alone in that bed to wake up to divorce papers, without even a fucking goodbye, so you'll have to forgive me for not thinking much of your word."

Head and heart aching, throat tight with unshed tears, she shoved by him and stalked inside, leaving him in the dark without another word.

GOD HELP HIM, she was crying.

Griff heard the muffled sounds of Sam weeping as he stood outside her door. He'd have preferred being shot again to knowing he was the cause of it. Everything in him wanted to go to her, to offer comfort, but he knew she wouldn't take it. So he stood for long minutes with his palm pressed to the door, feeling utterly useless.

It was only when she quieted that he slunk off to his own room for a long and restless night to wrestle with the fact that he'd hurt her so much worse than he'd imagined.

They'd been so young. And he'd been so full of the need to prove himself, to earn the unquestioning faith she had in him. He'd never thought he might have destroyed that faith in the process. That he'd betrayed that gift, that she saw his actions as callous rather than the well-intentioned sacrifice they'd been, kept him awake long after the rest of the wedding party stumbled to their beds. But it didn't stop him from waking with the sun.

The scent of coffee drew him to the kitchen, where he found Ari's dad, Flynn, sliding trays of muffins in the oven while his youngest daughter, Bailey, hurled cereal from her highchair.

The Irishman heaved a sigh. "Sure, and you're leaving more of that on the floor than you're stuffing in your face."

"You know she hates cereal when there's the option for something baked," Ari pointed out.

"This one wasn't born with a lick of patience, and I'm after keeping her quiet so her mother can sleep."

The toddler flashed a toothy, cherubic smile and threw another fistful of Cheerios in Griff's direction. He caught one and popped it in his mouth.

"Not even honey nut. Can't say I blame you, kid."

"You're up early. Did we wake you?" Flynn asked.

"My body clock is permanently dialed to waking at oh dark thirty."

"There will be muffins in about half an hour. Or I can make some bacon and eggs."

"Just coffee for now."

As it still felt odd being waited on in the house that had been a home, he crossed to the cabinet and retrieved a mug himself, pouring a cup of the rich brew. This was one of Joan's traditions that his sisters had kept when they opened the inn. She'd dearly loved her coffee and always splurged on high-quality beans. He considered carrying the mug out to the porch, but found himself sliding onto one of the long benches at the massive, scarred farmhouse table. Joan was no longer here to dole out advice, but he'd had enough time alone with his thoughts during the night. The company of family would keep him distracted. Closing his eyes, Griff sipped, savoring the dark flavor.

"Y'all were up awfully late last night," Ari observed.

"Lots of catching up to do. A lot of us haven't seen each other in years."

"Some unexpected reunions there, I'm guessing."

Griff frowned at the girl, wondering at the lively curiosity in her dark eyes. "I suppose so."

"Lots of walking down memory lane."

"That seems to be Kendrick and Erin's theme for the weekend."

She hummed a noncommittal note that he didn't trust for a minute.

"What?"

"Nothing. It's just... I never would have pegged you for getting married in Vegas."

Griff fixed her with a stare that had cowed lesser men. "You were eavesdropping?"

"I don't think it can be called eavesdropping when y'all were so loud." She lifted her own mug, sipped. "None of them realize it's Sam, do they?"

"You *were* eavesdropping." The idea that she'd been lurking in the dark, listening in on his conversation with Samantha, had his temper stirring.

"I didn't have to. I saw the look on both your

faces when you laid eyes on each other. It was easy enough to put two and two together. But thanks for the confirmation."

Well, he'd played right into that one.

Griff glanced at Flynn, who tried valiantly to hide his own curiosity. "Your daughter is a menace."

"She's a romantic heart and a poor sense of boundaries."

Sam had once been that kind of romantic. But he'd seen no signs of the soft-hearted girl he'd known in the woman who'd faced off with him last night. He was deathly afraid that was on him, too.

"So what happened?" Ari prompted. "And don't just say it's complicated. That was obvious."

As if he was going to spill his guts to a six-teen-year-old girl?

"Not your business, kid. And don't you go poking at Sam about it either. If she'd wanted anyone to know, she'd have said something herself."

"But—"

"No one's askin' you to play matchmaker, *cailín beag.*"

The clatter of feet on the stairs put an end to the discussion, such as it was. Kendrick came wandering in, looking far more awake than he had any right to.

"You're all bright-eyed and bushy-tailed, considering how late the bonfire ran," Griff observed.

"I am high on love, man. And excited about today." He made a beeline for the coffeepot.

"What exactly are we doing?"

"This morning we've got a scavenger hunt, of sorts. Then this afternoon the women have a bunch of spa time and the rest of us men will have a pick-up game of basketball. And tonight, we've got a tasting party out at the cidery."

"Because we didn't imbibe enough of Ryder's product last night?"

Kendrick dropped onto the opposite bench. "It's damned good cider."

Griff only grunted. "What's the deal with the scavenger hunt?"

"Since Erin and I both ended up back at the high school where we fell in love, she had the bright idea that we pair everyone off in teams—one groomsman, one bridesmaid—to hunt up all the places that were pivotal to our first relationship. We figured it'd be a good bonding activity for all the pairs who are walking down the aisle together."

"Please, for the love of all that is holy, tell me I'm not paired with Cressida."

"Nope. That questionable honor goes to Mick as best man. You're with Sam." He smiled into his coffee. "Erin and I always suspected you had a thing for your tutor. Since you're both single, we figured it couldn't hurt to give you a little nudge."

A choking laugh from Ari had Griff shooting a glare in her direction. She covered her amusement with a coughing fit that probably fooled no one.

"Sorry. Went down the wrong pipe. I'm just

gonna go do a thing." With a vague gesture to the door, she abandoned the table.

Flynn skillfully turned the conversation, buying Griff some time to finish his coffee, get his brain fully online. He'd be spending the morning with Sam, away from the others. Would they get the chance to talk, for him to explain himself? Would she listen if he did? He'd have to play it by ear, see how she reacted. He could bide his time. Maybe now that she was past the initial shock of seeing him, she'd be open to… something.

And maybe flying pigs will be the afternoon's entertainment.

The one thing he knew with absolute certainty was that she'd hate this scavenger hunt.

The rest of the wedding party began to wander in as Flynn piled warm muffins into a basket. "Muffins are here. For those of you with sore heads, have a glass what's in the pitcher there. It'll help you face the day."

As Mick, Mariko, and Roxanne queued up at the counter, Griff spotted Sam in the kitchen doorway, eyes heavy from sleep, her hair gathered into a loose braid that draped over one shoulder. The sight made him want to cuddle her, wrapping her up to protect her from what was coming today. Instead, he rose, skirting the others to pour a fresh cup of coffee, doctoring it with cream and sugar as he remembered she liked before crossing the room to press it into her hands.

Her brows drew together as she squinted up at him. "What—?"

"You're gonna need it," he murmured.

Erin bounced in, as bright and bubbly as her husband to be. "Good morning, beautiful people! Who's ready for a scavenger hunt?"

CHAPTER 4

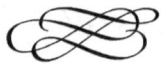

Sam shut the door to Griff's SUV and stared across the mostly empty parking lot at the red brick building where she'd counted down the days like a prison sentence. "This is hell. I'm in hell."

"Is it really that bad?"

She glared at him over the hood. "This place housed most of my greatest humiliations. I successfully avoided our ten-year reunion, only to be dragged back for this sham of a bonding exercise. No part of me wants to be here. There's literally *nothing* about high school I want to remember."

He studied her with that infuriatingly un-readable expression. "Would it be better if you were here with someone other than me?"

Part of her wanted to strike out and claim he was the worst part of the whole situation. It wasn't like she was thrilled to be paired up with him for the morning. But he hadn't tried to push conversation or talk about the past as they'd worked their way through Erin and Kendrick's list of firsts—grabbing photos of the bench in the city park where they'd had their first kiss and shots of the sign for the upcoming Apple Festival where they'd had their first date all those years ago—and unlike Cressida, it wasn't in her to be mean and spiteful. "No. Maybe Jill. Her high school years weren't any better than mine. It was why we were best friends. But of course, she's still not here."

Pocketing the keys, he moved around to the front of the SUV. "It's early yet. If she had plans last night, it'd take a few hours to get here from

Atlanta. Maybe she'll make it for the spa sessions this afternoon."

"Maybe."

Sam appreciated that he was trying to offer some comfort without dismissing her concerns. It might have worked if anyone had heard *anything* from Jill, but all was still radio silence on that front.

"We can go. Skip this whole thing. I'm not any more excited to trip down memory lane than you are."

"Not eager to relive the glory days?"

A muscle jumped in his jaw. "They weren't glory days. You know that."

Yeah. She did. She'd been one of the few to see that, even back then.

"Erin and Kendrick expect us to cooperate."

"Doesn't mean we have to. This isn't a test. Isn't even a real competition. We don't have to follow the rules. We can get the hell out of here." There was none of the judgment or rancor so often aimed at her for her tendency to follow the rules. Just a simple statement that there was an alternative.

"And do what?"

He jerked his shoulders. "I don't know. Find somewhere to talk, away from everybody."

Sam wanted to do that even less than she wanted to face her high school demons. "Pass. Let's get this over with."

Griff pursed his lips and nodded in easy acceptance. He beat her to the door, tugging it open for her. "Looks like Erin and Kendrick unlocked things for us."

"I wonder where they are."

"I wouldn't put it past them to be making out in her classroom and fulfilling some kind of hot for teacher fantasies."

Sam blinked, his words sending her mind back to Vegas, to another friend's wedding, where Griff had agreed to be her fake boyfriend and plus one. He'd claimed to have had hot for teacher fantasies about her during their tutoring sessions. She'd assumed he'd made it up for the sake of their cover, and damn, he'd sold it, reeling off quotes from Shelley until she'd wanted to climb into his lap right there at the dinner table.

Shrugging off the memory, she moved past him, into the dim halls of the school. He entered behind her, letting the door swing shut with a clang. He didn't invade her space, but she knew precisely where he stood. His mere presence pulled at her like a frigging gravitational field. Her awareness of him hadn't dimmed one iota in the last eight years, and Sam hated it. He'd had this effect on her since middle school. She should've outgrown it by now.

"Where to?" The quiet rumble of his voice seemed to echo in the empty hall.

"Their first I love you was under the bleachers at the football field. And they first became official in the gym."

"Gym first. How do you even remember all this stuff?"

"Girls talk about this kind of thing a lot more than guys, and I used to be a romantic."

She pretended not to notice his sharp look

in her direction. Acknowledging that he was the reason she'd given up on love for herself would open the door to that discussion she refused to have. It wasn't like she'd declared never ever, but sooner or later—usually sooner—any guys who'd tried to date her had cottoned to her Titanic-sized trust issues. She expected them to leave, so they usually did. If she let them believe those issues stemmed from her absentee father, well, it was a convenient stereotype that let her avoid discussing the truth.

Sam hesitated at the doorway to the gym, one hand on the bar. The room beyond was dark, lit only by the faint red glow of exit signs. Just the sight of it had her heart rate tripping.

"Samantha?"

Swallowing hard, she dropped her hand and stepped back. "Do you know where the light switch is?" Damn it, she hadn't been able to keep the hitch from her voice.

"I think there's one just inside the door. What's wrong?"

"I need you to go turn it on." She couldn't go in there in the dark. Not again.

His heavy gaze was full of questions, but he merely nodded. "Okay."

At the metallic clank of the bar and the squeak of the hinge, her chest went tight. Damn it, she was thirty years old. She shouldn't be having a panic attack over this half a lifetime later. But she hadn't quite gotten her breathing under control by the time Griff slipped back out of the now illuminated gym.

He swore, wrapping an arm around her shoulders and steering her back toward the entrance. "No scavenger hunt is worth this."

Sam dug in her heels. "I'm fine."

"You're about to hyperventilate."

"I'm not letting her still have power over me." She wished he didn't either. Every cell of her body wanted to lean into the warmth and strength of him. Instead, she pulled away, shoving through the door herself and scanning the space.

The gym hadn't changed much since her

tenure at Eden's Ridge High School. Wooden bleachers were retracted up against opposite walls on either side of the basketball court. The larger-than-life painted mascot still snarled from one wall. But the court itself was blessedly empty. No one was lurking in the dark to terrorize her now. She took one breath, then another, willing her pulse to slow.

"What happened, Sam?"

She could've put him off, refused to explain. But the fear still felt raw and close to the surface. "Junior year, I got a note from you asking to meet me here after I got out of some club meeting I had that day."

His brows drew together. "I never asked to meet you here."

"I didn't know that then. I figured you wanted to go over some stuff for a test after football practice and that's why you'd picked the gym. When I got here, it was dark. I didn't see them before they were on me."

His battle-hardened body went rigid beside her, his hands balled to fists. "Who?"

Because she needed to stay calm, she kept her recitation flat and emotionless. "Not a hundred percent sure of all of them. But Cressida, for sure. I'll never forget her laughing. They knocked me down, wrapped me up in one of the big volleyball nets, and shoved me in the storage closet with the other equipment. Coach Cobb found me hours later. I still have nightmares about being confined."

Griff's blue eyes were incandescent with rage. "How was this not all over school? How was she not expelled?"

She shrugged. "The administration couldn't do anything. I didn't actually *see* who attacked me. There was no clear evidence, no way to prove it. And Cressida's dad was golf buddies with the principal."

"She terrorized you."

"Yes. For years." It was a simple statement of fact, not an intentional twist of the knife of guilt.

He scrubbed a hand over his face. "I didn't know. I swear to God, I didn't know."

Hating his expression of self-loathing, she couldn't quite stop herself from lifting a hand to his cheek. "I know. I never blamed you."

"Why the hell didn't you tell me?"

"Because it would have made things worse. You'd have confronted her, and whether you broke up with her or not—"

"I sure as fuck would have." The vehement declaration didn't mean anything. It couldn't.

"She'd have continued her harassment either way."

"Fuck." He laced his hands behind his head and paced three restless steps away. "Fuck!"

"You wouldn't have been able to protect me. And anyway, Jonah took care of it. She didn't come after me physically after that."

Griff dropped his arms. "I knew she sniped at you, but I never thought... I'm sorry. Christ, I'm so sorry."

"They weren't your actions to apologize for. But tell me this—because I've always wondered —What the hell did you see in her?"

His shoulders slumped, curled in obvious shame. "She was easy."

Sam went brows up. "Well, that's blunt."

His eyes came back to hers. "I didn't mean like that."

"Didn't you? She spent enough time talking about your sex life."

"To you?" Fresh horror dawned on his face.

"To anyone who'd listen. But yeah, she took particular joy in rubbing it in my face that you wanted her."

"I didn't."

She crossed her arms. "You're saying you didn't sleep with her?"

Color crept up his cheeks above his beard, and he couldn't quite meet her eyes. "I was a selfish, stupid teenage boy who didn't say no to what was offered. But I didn't want her. She didn't matter. That's why being with her was easy. I didn't have to be careful or watch myself. She was... a placeholder."

Sam just stared at him. "That is the most asinine reason for a relationship I think I've ever heard."

"That's one of a whole lot of things from back then that I'm not proud of. I wasn't a good guy. God, I told you that in Vegas. But I've done everything in my power to change that."

Sam frowned. "That wasn't who you were. Or at least not all you were." She wouldn't have loved him if that had been the case.

"You were one of the only ones to think so."

And she'd changed the course of his life because of it. No matter what had happened in Vegas, she couldn't regret that.

His eyes darkened, and he took a step toward her. "Samantha..."

Straightening her shoulders, she stepped back. "Let's get this picture and get going."

* * *

"I KNOW I've got my old high school yearbooks in here somewhere." Sam slapped on the light switch and stepped into the room. "They're bound to give us some clues for the last picture."

Griff hung back a bit, unsure whether he was supposed to follow her into her childhood bedroom. As much time as he'd spent in this house, he'd never been back here. All their study sessions had taken place in the little kitchen or somewhere on campus. Even back then, he'd known that Jonah would've throttled him for being in his sister's bedroom, no matter how innocent the circumstances. But they weren't kids anymore and curiosity drove him over the threshold.

"So this is the inner sanctum."

Sam paused in her riffling through the shelves and glanced at the room. "Yeah. It hasn't been updated much since I left."

He wasn't sure what he'd expected. Maybe something frilly and girly to go along with the romantic nature she'd had. A muted plaid spread echoed the soft green of the walls. Floor-to-ceiling bookshelves marched along two walls and brimmed with books of every stripe. He'd always imagined she'd be ruthlessly organized with her books, but the shelves were a cheerful jumble of rows and stacks and knick-knacks. A sturdy desk was shoved into one corner, and he could just imagine a teenage Sam sitting in the chair, head bent over a book as she took notes. The only artwork seemed to be framed quotes, arranged gallery style around the full-sized bed. They'd been printed in varying fonts, set off in simple, black dollar-store frames. She'd always carried a notebook where she scribbled down lines and passages she loved. Stepping closer, he skimmed some of them, recognizing lines from Byron, Shakespeare, and Keats. There were others he didn't recognize. And then one he did.

For it was not into my ear you whispered, but into my heart. It was not my lips you kissed, but my soul. - Judy Garland

Griff lifted a hand to rub at his chest where the first half of the quote was inked. The sentiment hadn't changed in all these years, and seeing her again made him feel every one of their years apart like a fresh bruise. The ache went beyond skin deep, and suddenly he couldn't stop himself from pressing, just a little.

"I was always coming back for you."

The sound of shifting books stopped, and he turned to find her staring at him, exasperation and disbelief etched on her face.

"If you were going to come back, you've apparently had ample time. You don't have to lie about it to make me feel better. You made a promise in that letter that was every bit as impulsive as our marriage, and you grew up. It's fine." She turned back to the bookshelves.

Yeah, Griff was well aware they were anything but fine. He crossed the small room in two strides, touching her shoulder where he knew the other half of the quote lived in her skin and hating the stiffness he found there. "I'm not lying, Samantha. I made a promise, and I meant it."

The breath she exhaled sounded strained. "Why do you keep bringing this up? You ended things."

"I did what I thought was best at the time. I didn't expect you to wait for me. But I sure as hell want to know if what we felt is still there."

She turned, throwing up her hands in frustration. "To what end?"

"If there's still something here after all these years, it seems to me that's something worth exploring, intentionally, as mature adults."

There were shades of the flustered girl he'd known in the hands she lifted and dropped. "What do you want from me, Griff?"

She didn't seem exactly receptive, but none of her answers had been "Leave me the hell alone," so he decided to take the shot. "One kiss." He wanted a lot more than that, but this was all he'd ask for now. "If there's nothing there, then we know, and I'll never say another word about it."

On an impatient huff, she crossed her arms. "Fine." She lifted her face and waited, dark eyes cool.

She clearly expected this to be a fast nothing, but Griff wasn't about to waste the opportunity. This might be the last time he ever got to kiss her, and he intended to make the most of it.

Stepping close enough to feel her heat, he lifted his hands, indulging himself by combing his fingers through her hair. God, it was soft. He remembered the feel of it in his hands, the tantalizing brush of it over his chest as she rode him. The memory made him stir, but he kept his touch slow and gentle, stroking his thumbs along her cheeks, absorbing the silk of her skin, until she let out the barest of sighs. Then he bent his mouth to hers, determined to find the spark he knew was still there and seduce her into a second chance.

She remained utterly still, her lips immobile against the play of his. He wondered if he'd misread her, blinded by his own yearning and the hope he'd clung to for years. Then his hand slid lower, his fingers brushing her throat, and he felt the frantic hammer of her pulse that belied her nonreactive stance. Emboldened, he cupped her nape and angled her head for better access, nibbling, sipping at her mouth until she trembled and opened for him.

The taste of her hit him like a mortar round, blowing away the last of his flimsy control. Griff hauled her closer, needing to feel her against him. She whimpered once, and he eased his hold, starting to lift his head. But as she'd done once long ago, she fisted her hands in his shirt and pulled him back, wrapping her arms around his neck and fusing her mouth with his in fevered demand.

Her surrender stoked his own madness, and he spun, backing her toward the bed until they tumbled onto it, a tangle of seeking limbs and desperate mouths. Christ, he needed to get closer. Needed to feel her. His hand snaked under her sweater, finding heated skin even as her hands went to his belt. Yes. God, yes. He wanted her naked and writhing beneath him.

Some sound penetrated the haze of lust, the situational awareness honed by his years in the Marines making him hesitate mere seconds before he stripped off her sweater.

"—baby, I didn't know you were stopping by."

Samantha froze for a split second, and they both heard the footsteps in the hall. Then they were struggling to untangle, pushing away from each other hard enough that they both crashed off opposite sides of the bed. Griff's elbow cracked against the desk, shooting pain up his arm.

The woman in the doorway was an older version of Sam, except for the sharp green eyes. She cleared her throat, her lips pursed in a smirk of amusement as she took in the pair of them on the floor.

Sam scrambled up, straightening her sweater and running a hand through the hair still mussed from his hands. "We were just, um, looking for my old yearbooks."

Her mom nodded with wide, sure-I-believe-you eyes. "Is that what the kids are calling it these days? Hello, Griff."

"Ma'am." His ears burned, and he thanked God that a beard covered most of his face.

Sam had no such benefit. A crimson flush crept up from her neck to her hairline, replacing the heat of passion.

"Well, I just wanted to let you know I was home. I'll just leave you to your… search. There are cookies in the jar in the kitchen." With that, her mom pointedly shut the door.

For long moments, they stayed where they were, saying nothing as footsteps retreated down the hall.

At last, Sam dropped her head in her hands. "How is it that feels just as mortifying now as it would have at seventeen?"

"There is no statute of limitations on parental embarrassment." And they had been making out like a couple of horny teenagers, too stupid to even think about closing the damned door.

"True story."

Smoothing her hair, she circled the bed and resumed searching the shelves.

Griff stayed where he was for a few minutes, struggling to get himself under control. The last thing he needed was to walk past Rebecca Ferguson, still sporting a hard-on for her daughter. Not that there'd been a single doubt about what they'd been up to. Hell, maybe the no bedroom rule had been a good one for this house.

Except he wouldn't give up that kiss for anything. It was proof that the hope he'd clung to all these years wasn't pure self-delusion.

Sam pulled a book off the shelf. "Found it."

Oh, hell no. He wouldn't go back to before and pretend that kiss hadn't happened. Shoving to his feet, he crossed over, gently turning her to face him. "There's still something here."

She stared up at him, her eyes searching his face for long moments, and he wondered if she'd try to deny it or say it didn't matter.

Instead, she surprised him by blowing out a breath. "Apparently so."

CHAPTER 5

"*I* should have known Ryder would have the inside track on all things about your relationship back then," Mariko complained. "Declan and I didn't have a prayer."

Roxanne, who'd been paired up with Ryder, relaxed back in the pedicure chair with a satisfied sigh. "Easy as shooting fish in a barrel. We even had time to grab coffee at the diner."

Sam didn't really give a damn that she and Griff hadn't won. She had plenty of more important concerns. Like what the hell she was going to do about the fact that there was very much still something between her and her ex-husband. Odd that she thought of him like that when he'd been her husband so briefly.

They were still hot for each other. That wasn't really a surprise. Chemistry wasn't rational, and it rarely faded with time. She wasn't delusional enough to kick herself for responding. Not when she'd wanted him the moment she'd seen him again. The smart play would have been to shut him down when he'd asked for the kiss. But a part of her had needed to know if she'd inflated her memory of how they'd been together. If anything, it had dimmed over the years. They were explosive. She'd been one hundred percent ready to ignore all the hurt and pain and betrayal just to have him again. And that was a level of stupid she couldn't handle.

Thank God they'd been interrupted. Not that she'd be able to look her mother in the eye for at least a year. Being not a stupid woman, Rebecca had known about her crush back in high school. It had been an open secret that most everyone had known about. But her mom didn't know about Vegas. No one did. So there was no telling what she'd thought about what she'd walked in on. Sam had hustled Griff out the door with barely more than a wave, and she didn't intend to give her mom an opportunity to share her opinion.

"Just relax back now." Nadia Flores eased the treatment chair horizontal. "We're going to do a nice, moisturizing facial."

Sam tried to do as she asked, but the moment she closed her eyes and felt the gentle sweep of Nadia's fingers over her cheeks, it was Griff's phantom touch she remembered. He'd been so... careful with her. His capacity for gentleness had staggered and frustrated her at twenty-two. She'd wanted to believe she'd imagined that, too. Wanted to stand firm in the face of his unrelenting assault on her senses. But she was only human, and he made her feel alive and cherished in a way no one else ever had.

"So how did things go with Griff today?"

At Erin's question, Sam's eyes flew open. "How did what go with Griff?" Damn it, her voice was squeaking. That wasn't obvious at all.

"So it's still like that, huh?"

Despite the smile in Erin's tone, Sam didn't reply until she felt certain she could modulate her voice. "Like what?"

"He always made you nervous."

"A man who looks like that doesn't make you nervous, you'd best have somebody checking to make sure you still have a pulse," Roxanne declared.

Echoes of agreement sounded all over the room from the bridal party and technicians alike.

"You're both single," Erin continued. "I thought pairing you up together might give things a little... you know... nudge between you."

Yeah, a nudge right off the Cliffs of Insanity.

"Oh, come on. As if Griff would ever go for someone like her. He's not into the brainy type."

Sam started to curl her hands before she remembered the manicure. Cressida was so sure she knew him. What would she say if she knew he'd married Sam? If she knew she hadn't mattered to him, but that he still wanted this brainiac? The words were on the tip of her tongue, but she held them back. She prided herself on not being deliberately vicious. Letting loose would lower her to Cressida's level. Besides, what good would it do to open that can of worms? She didn't know what she was going to do about him, and there was no need to complicate the situation by bringing in anyone else's opinions.

"Oh stuff it, Cressida. Nobody asked you. He'd be lucky to have someone like Sam."

Cressida didn't quite hold in a sniff. "Yeah, well, there's a big difference between walking on the wild side back in the day and doing it as a grown adult. He's never been what you'd call dependable."

Temper flared, and all Sam's protective instincts ran roughshod over her good sense. "Griffin has always shown up for the people who mattered, something you'd be aware of if you knew him at all. But you never considered him a person. He was only ever a conquest to you. That's how you've always operated, and it's no surprise that you're still the same petty social climber who believes the world revolves around you as you always were. The rest of us grew the hell up."

At the weighted silence that followed, Sam closed her eyes and her mouth. She hadn't meant to say so much.

"Mrs. Milton, you're due up for your massage. This way, please."

As Pru escorted a fuming Cressida out of the room, Sam loosed a breath.

"Well, damn," Mariko muttered. "If my nails weren't wet, I'd totally give you a high five."

"Pretty sure you just lived out several people's high school fantasies," Roxanne added. "You go, girl!"

The solidarity was only a little comforting. She'd just fired back at her nemesis, and she knew perfectly well that never ended in anything other than her own bloodshed.

"I'm sorry, Erin. I promised myself I wouldn't antagonize her."

"Oh, don't mind me, honey. She's only here through family blackmail. Don't feel obligated to hold back on my account."

Well, it was nice to have her friend's support, for what it was worth. "Still, I don't want to make things awkward at your wedding."

"She'll do that all by herself. I'm hoping she'll finally show her ass in a public enough fashion that my mother will stop expecting me to include her in anything. And anyway, it doesn't matter. At the end of the day, all I care about is that I'm finally marrying the man I love."

Sam wished her own wants were that clear. But one thing was certain—for better or worse, Griffin was back in her life, and she had some major decisions to make.

"So... can we talk about the more interesting part of that outburst?" Mariko asked. "It totally sounds like you were a lot closer to him than any of us realized."

You have no idea. "I saw him one-on-one, away from all the social groups who expected him to behave a certain way, so I saw a side other than the wild child. He talked to me."

She'd treasured those conversations, all those little pockets of time alone with the real him. That had been the guy she'd fallen for long before they'd reconnected in Vegas. That had been the guy she'd gone out on a limb for when he'd gotten in over his head with one too many bad decisions. She couldn't deny she was seeing shades of him in the man he'd become.

"He's definitely not the wild child anymore after all that time in the military," Erin observed. "Who would've thought he, of all people, would choose the Marines?"

When the choice had been jail or the military, there wasn't an actual decision to make. That, too, had been on Sam. When Griff had been arrested as part of a robbery that had gotten out of hand, she'd convinced the judge to give him the option, to give him one last chance to prove he was a better man than the company he'd kept. Griff hadn't known, not until Vegas. If she hadn't told him, would he have felt driven to re-enlist to prove himself? Would he have even married her to begin with? Those were the questions she hadn't let herself ponder much over the years. No sense in torturing herself with something she couldn't know the answer to.

Uncomfortable with the direction of conversation, she changed the subject. "I know I've been sounding like a broken record on this front, but has anyone heard from Jill? She should have been here long before now if she was coming."

"Not a peep. I texted and called this morning, but nothing." Erin's tone was far too casual.

"Aren't you worried?"

"I wish I could say it was unusual, but it's not. We've made plans several times over the years that have fallen through, for one reason or another. I don't hold it against her. She's always marched to the beat of her own drum, and I know she'll be here for the wedding. That's the part that matters."

Maybe Erin was right, and everything was fine, but Sam wasn't content with making assumptions. As soon as she was done with these spa treatments, she had some digging to do.

AFTER LUNCH, Ryder disappeared to the cidery to do setup for the evening's festivities, and Griff piled into Kendrick's SUV with Mick and Declan. Conversation flowed around him, full of the jovial bullshitting of brothers and friends, but he couldn't pay attention. His mind was too full of Sam and that kiss. He wished like hell they hadn't been interrupted. They understood each other in bed, and it seemed like they'd be closer to on the same page if they'd managed to finish what they'd started. At least he'd secured an acknowledgment from her that there was still something between them. But it wasn't enough. Not without confirmation that she was willing to deliberately pursue it.

When they'd come together in Vegas, it had been fast and impulsive. He'd been the king of fast and impulsive back in the day, but the leap had been totally out of character for her. She'd want time to think about this, consider the angles. Decide whether she could trust him again. She deserved the time, but he knew there was a very real possibility that once this weekend was over, his chance might be, too. How much should he push her?

Kendrick whipped his Explorer into the high school parking lot.

Griff tensed. "What are we doing back here?"

"There's rain in the forecast this afternoon, so I figured we'd have our pickup game here instead of the park. Being a teacher doesn't have too many perks, but easy access to the court is one."

It was hard to look at the gym the same after what Sam had told him this morning.

Griff scanned the room, wondering where Cressida and her cronies had hidden for the ambush, and which closet it had been. Had a single one of the people involved felt a shred of remorse? It had been nearly fifteen years and Sam had still come damned close to a full-blown panic attack today, just walking into the room. How much worse must it have been when it happened? The idea of her bound, alone in the dark, terrified, made him want to break something.

"Hey, man, you okay?"

At the sound of Declan's voice, Griff jolted, trying to pull his mind back to the now.

He'd known Cressida was a verbal bully and had done nothing, believing that making Sam seem unimportant to him would keep her from being as much of a target. God, he'd been an idiot. How much more had he missed? The boy he'd been had ignored a problem. The man he was needed to know.

"Did y'all ever hear about Cressida bullying Sam?"

Looks were exchanged that had Griff's gut tightening in dread.

Kendrick was the one who broke the stand-off. "Dude, she wasn't exactly subtle in the shit she said."

"I don't mean verbally. I mean physically."

Mick grabbed a basketball from the rack and began to dribble. "Cressida always struck me as someone who'd be afraid she'd break a nail. But she's mean-spirited enough to recruit others to do her dirty work, I expect. Why?"

"Something Sam told me about today. I wondered if there were more incidents I didn't know about."

"I don't know, man. Girls are usually more devious in their bullying, so they don't get caught as easily. The shit I've seen some of them pull since I've been a teacher is enough to make me go gray." Kendrick studied him. "You're really upset about this."

Griff shook his head. "I should have done something."

"Like what?" Declan asked. "I mean, short of

having better taste in women than Cressida in the first place."

"I don't know. She's just one of a long line of shit decisions I made back then. Been confronting a lot of those." Trying to shrug off the mood, he darted in and snatched the ball from Mick. "C'mon, let's play. I need to move."

They paired off, Mick and Kendrick against Griff and Declan. For an aggressive half hour, they played. Griff worked off some of the impotent rage in sprints from one end of the court to the other. Settling into the rhythm of the game and the familiar trash talk, he felt some of the tension loosen.

At the break, Declan flopped right down on the floor, gasping. "Shit, I'm getting too old for this, y'all."

Griff handed him a bottle of water.

Declan glared at him. "I'm trying real hard not to be mortally offended by the fact that you're not even breathing hard."

"If you'd spent the last twelve years dodging bullets, you wouldn't be breathing hard either.

But you wouldn't have that sweet kid of yours, so I'd say you came out on the better end of that."

"Fair point." He guzzled down half the bottle. "You had a break in there somewhere, right? After your first stint?"

"Not a long one. I re-upped when I was twenty-two."

"Crazy to think where we all were back then. Mariko and I were talking about it earlier today. I was raising a toddler on my own. She'd just been accepted to law school. I guess most everybody else who did the college thing was graduating about then." Declan sipped more water. "Well, Sam didn't. Mariko mentioned she'd graduated a year early and jumped on into that PhD program."

"She always was smart as hell," Mick observed. "Totally not surprised she became a professor."

Griff grunted and dribbled the ball, moving into position to practice some layups.

Kendrick moved with him, automatically

falling into a guarding stance. "She mentioned her Vegas wedding was at the start of grad school. That would've been about the same time as yours, wouldn't it?"

Griff pivoted, putting his back to his brother as he positioned for the shot. "Your point?"

"Nothing. I just think it's interesting, is all. It's not like you married each other."

Griff's shoes screeched as he stumbled to a halt and the ball shot out of his hand, bouncing out of reach.

Kendrick's eyes peeled wide as he pointed with both hands. "Holy shit! You *did* marry each other! Dude!"

"Are you fucking serious?" Mick demanded.

"I *knew* I sensed a vibe with you two." Declan scrambled to his feet.

He ought to shut all this down, get them back to the game. But the window for denial had already passed. And maybe a part of him wanted to finally tell *somebody*. "Okay, yes, we got married in Vegas when we were twenty-two."

Mick grinned. "Was it one of those crazy drunk weddings with Elvis officiating?"

"No. It was entirely on purpose." And he'd meant for it to be forever.

Kendrick crossed his arms. "But you're not still married."

"No."

"What happened?" Declan asked.

His own self-doubts had gotten the better of him. "I fucked it up." He realized that now. He'd fucked up so many things in his life. He couldn't afford to do the same with this second chance.

"Shit. So when she said that stuff about closure last night, she was talking about you?"

"Probably." Griff didn't intend to give her the kind of closure she was looking for. He wasn't walking away from her again without a fight. "Look, you can't say anything to anybody. I'm trying to fix what I broke, and Sam's liable to spook if anybody gives her shit about this. Your word, all of you."

"But—" Kendrick began.

"Silence, my brother. Not even your future wife can know. This is as serious as that thing from senior year that we do not speak of."

All three of them straightened, understanding the gravity of the situation.

At last, Kendrick nodded. "Fine. My lips are sealed."

"Nice to know your taste has improved a lot since high school. I'll keep the secret," Mick promised.

"Won't tell a soul," Declan added. "But I feel like it's our brotherly duty to ask what we can do to help the cause."

"Kendrick's already done it, pairing us up for the wedding. Convincing her she can trust me again is entirely on me."

And he had no idea how he was going to pull that off.

CHAPTER 6

Something was wrong.

Sam could feel it in her bones. Between the spa sessions that hadn't done a damned thing to relax her and getting ready for tonight's party, she'd done a deep dive into Jill's social media, trying to unearth some clue to where she was and what was going on. What she'd found had been a big, fat nothing. Jill didn't use any particular service regularly, and there'd been no posts at all in nearly a week. The last activity Sam had been able to find was a thumbs up to one of Erin's posts about the upcoming bachelorette party weekend on Thursday, which suggested she'd been planning to come at that point.

So where the hell was she, and why wasn't she answering anybody?

Sam couldn't focus on Ryder's husband Lewis as he discussed tasting notes about the flight of ciders in front of her. Just sitting here for the night, as if everything was fine, felt wrong on every possible level. Maybe she was the only one of the group who remembered the occasions in high school when the reason Jill hadn't shown had been because she very definitely wasn't okay. Jill had been adept at hiding the bruises, and people were good at forgetting any unpleasantness that didn't touch them directly.

What if Jill had gone by to see her father? She'd never totally cut him off, despite the abuse. Sam had always questioned the wisdom of that, but Jill had insisted he was her only family and that somebody had to check on him. Was he even still in Eden's Ridge?

"What are you thinking?"

Sam couldn't stop a shudder at the low rumble of Griff's voice near her ear. "Nothing."

"Professor, you've never thought nothing in your entire life. Try again."

Accurate. But even so, he'd obviously been watching her, and she'd been too preoccupied to notice. She considered putting him off, but he'd only keep pushing. "I was just wondering if Rick Dunham was still in Eden's Ridge."

Griff blinked, his mouth pulling into a frown as he considered the implications.

In all probability, she was overreacting. But now that the idea had lodged itself in her mind, she couldn't leave this stone unturned. She shoved back from the table, the scrape of her chair drawing everyone's attention. "I'm sorry. I need to go."

Erin frowned. "Is everything okay, honey?"

"Yeah, it's fine. I just… have to go. There's something I need to take care of. I'll meet you back at the inn. Lewis, I apologize for the interruption. It was lovely to see you again."

"You, too, sweet cheeks. Take care."

Griff stood as she grabbed her purse. "Wait up."

"What?" She cast an uneasy glance at the avid curiosity of the rest of the wedding party.

"I'm coming with you."

"Excuse me?"

"If you're doing what I think you're doing, you're sure as fuck not doing it alone." His easy tone masked utter implacability.

Mick snickered. "That's what she said."

Someone thumped him. "Shut up."

Sam didn't dare look at the rest of the wedding party. Her attention was firmly on Griff. Arguing with him would only stoke further questions from the others, and truth be told, the hollow was a dicey place to wander in the daytime. There'd been more than one meth lab bust in the area over the years, not to mention an assortment of other crime associated with extreme poverty. Having a former Marine as a bodyguard wasn't a bad idea. Especially as he'd grown up there himself before going into foster care.

"Fine. But I'm driving."

They strode out of the cidery together, the weight of everybody's stares on their backs.

"They're going to ask questions," she murmured.

"Don't give a damn. I failed to protect you once. I won't make that mistake again."

The grim promise in his voice had her glancing up in surprise. He'd obviously been thinking about what she'd admitted about Cressida this morning, and it didn't sit well. "I wasn't yours to protect then."

"You should've been."

Well, that was a rabbit hole she didn't dare go down. Instead, she picked up the pace. "I'm not yours to protect now, either."

"Agree to disagree. You've got no business going to the holler on your own."

She tugged open her car door. "It's probably a long shot, but maybe he's heard from her, or maybe Jill stopped there on the way into town. I can't just sit here."

Griff only nodded and slid into the passenger seat. He remained silent as she drove away from the orchard and headed south.

"You think I'm being foolish."

"No. If you'd tried to shake me off and gone out there by yourself, that would've been foolish. But going to check just makes you a friend."

Some tension inside her loosened. "Thanks for that. It's killing me that nobody else seems concerned."

"Nobody else had an up-close-and-personal view of Jill's dad when he was on a bender. Or the aftermath. It didn't occur to me she'd go back there. I sure as hell haven't been back since I left."

Sam dared a glance over at him, but he was watching the road. "Is your dad still there?"

"Hell if I know. We haven't spoken since high school, and I can't say as the interactions we had then were friendly. The last time I saw him, he'd shown up at Joan's wanting to drag me back to that hellhole. He was ranting and carrying on, and she just stood there, calm as you please, telling him if he set foot back on her property, he'd be met with the business end of a shotgun." He loosed a short laugh. "Damn, I loved that woman."

"I was sorry to hear she passed."

"Yeah. Me, too. I didn't see enough of her in those last years."

Because he'd been overseas with the Marines, trying to prove himself. He'd never understood that he didn't have to earn love. Not from her; not from his foster mother. They'd seen his value from the beginning. But he'd made enough offhand comments during their tutoring sessions that she knew that hadn't been the message drilled into him at home. It had been her mistake to believe that she could overcome that early programming with the sheer magnitude of her love for him.

They lapsed back into silence until her headlights passed over the faded, graffiti-covered sign of Hyde's Hills Trailer Park. She turned onto the rutted gravel road. Tension radiated from Griff as he leaned forward, eyes scanning the weedy yards full of rusted-out cars and clotheslines. All the years she'd been friends with Jill, she'd only been out here a handful of times, and even then it was only for a pickup. She couldn't imagine living here. What kind of horrible memories was this little field trip dragging up for Griff?

"Turn right."

Following his direction, she bumped onto another, more washed-out lane. The units were closer together here, with ancient cars and trucks parked practically on the doorsteps. Many of the single-wide trailers were missing large chunks of flashing around the base, leaving gaping holes that somehow made Sam uneasy. As they rolled by, she saw curtains twitch in several windows. A man sat in a lawn chair on a rickety porch, something draped across his lap. The cigarette in his mouth glowed red as his gaze followed their progress.

"Was that a... gun in his lap?"

"Yep. Left up there at the end of the row."

Sam swallowed, suddenly very, very glad he'd insisted on accompanying her. She made the turn, jolting as a dog shot out from beneath the closest trailer, snarling and barking like a hound of hell. It drew up short as it reached the end of its chain.

Griff's hand settled on her leg, a comforting warmth. "I've got you. It's that greenish one there on the right."

Because she wanted to curl her fingers with his, she tightened her grip on the wheel. "I'm glad you remembered where you're going."

She parked in what amounted to the driveway, beside an eighties-era Lincoln that might once have been white but was now mostly rust. In the glow of the headlights, she could see a sag in the middle of the trailer, as if it were a swayback horse. One window was boarded up, and the other had duct tape following a long crack in the glass. A light glowed behind it.

"You can stay in the car." Griff reached for the door handle.

"No, I should come. He might respond better to me." Besides, she'd dragged Griff into this. The least she could do was follow through on her own damned mission.

They got out of the car. He hustled around, his gaze seeming to track everywhere at once as he took her hand. She wasn't about to argue. No matter what he'd done to her heart, she knew he'd protect her from any physical threat. Sticking close, she stepped up on the cinderblock steps with him, wincing as his fist rapped against the storm door. When no one answered after several seconds, he knocked again.

"Help you?" The pack-a-day smoker's voice rasped from behind them.

Griff easily shifted, nudging her behind him as he addressed the neighbor. "We're looking for Rick Dunham. This still his place?"

The woman tugged her housecoat tighter around her against the chill. "Yeah. He ain't home, though."

"Know where we can find him?"

She squinted, eying first them, then the car. "You the law?"

"No."

"Bill collectors?"

"No, ma'am. I grew up here."

The woman took a closer look. "You're Burt Powell's boy?"

"Yes, ma'am."

She brayed a ragged laugh and slapped the two-by-four that constituted her porch rail. "Well, don't that beat all? Wondered what happened to you. Grew up fine, now, didn't you?"

Sam edged out a little, wanting to get this back on track and save him from having to stay here any longer than necessary. "We're looking for a woman. My friend, Jill. Rick's daughter. Have you seen her?"

"Haven't seen no woman around. Leastwise, not one young enough to be his kid. You want to talk to him, he's probably up at The Right Attitude."

Sam tensed.

Of course he is. Because where else would repro-bates hang out than my father's bar?

Feeling a little queasy, she said nothing as Griff thanked the woman for her help and began herding her toward the car. When he tucked her into the passenger side, she didn't argue.

He slid behind the wheel, readjusting the seat to accommodate his long legs. "What do you want to do?"

"Well, you just had to face down some of your demons. Now I get to face down mine. Let's go."

GRIFF PULLED up to the squat cinderblock building, noting the collection of trucks and motorcycles in the gravel lot illuminated by the dull yellow glow of the lone sodium vapor light high on a wooden pole. He was willing to bet some were the same ones that had been here years ago, when he'd come to drag his old man home. It was a hard-drinking bar for a hard-drinking crowd.

Beside him, Samantha stared at the place with grim loathing. He'd felt her mounting anxiety with every mile. She and her mom and brother had been so cut off from Lonnie Barker, Griff hadn't even known the man was her father until she'd mentioned it all those years ago in Vegas. Were they still estranged?

"Are you worried you'll run into your dad?"

"No. He died six months ago." Her flat words fell between them like stones.

Griff didn't know what to say, but she kept speaking.

"This lovely establishment is technically half mine. Or will be, if there's anything left once probate is finished." She flashed a humorless smile. "What an inheritance, right? Sorry I didn't take care of you growing up. Here's the thing I actually cared most about."

Griff couldn't even imagine her inside, let alone as part owner of this place. "What will you and Jonah do with it?"

"I don't know. Sell it. Bulldoze it. Neither of us has any interest in keeping it open beyond getting the estate settled. We'll figure it out once he's finished up in Syracuse."

"What's he doing in Syracuse?" There was no naval base up there.

"A treatment and skills training program that will hopefully leave him in better shape than he was when he left the SEALs."

That sounded ominous. Griff was almost afraid to ask what had happened. "I always figured him for a lifer."

"So did he. The post-concussion syndrome had other ideas." She unfastened her seatbelt. "It was touch and go there for a bit. At this point, Mom and I are just glad he's safe, and we don't have to lose sleep wondering where he is and if he's okay. I'll sleep better knowing both of you are out."

She'd worried about him?

Before Griff could respond to that, she'd shoved open the door and slipped out. He hurried around the car and joined her, unable to stop himself from pressing a hand to the small of her back as he opened the heavy black door. It was as much need to touch her as a public claiming for all the men whose eyes swung toward her when they stepped inside. The din of conversation dropped until all they could hear was the crack of pool balls and the tinny country music blaring out of an ancient radio behind the long, scarred bar.

Sam edged closer, and it was natural as breathing to curve his fingers over her hip. This place likely hadn't seen anyone so classy as her in... maybe ever, as evidenced by the assortment of bras lining the walls like trophies. Griff had always wondered if they belonged to Lonnie's conquests or if the women donated them to the questionable cause of decorating.

"In the corner," Sam murmured.

Griff barely recognized Rick Dunham. Years of alcohol abuse had reddened his face and fattened his paunch. He sat alone at a battered round table, nursing a drink as he watched the game being played at the lone pool table.

Sam squared her shoulders and headed in his direction. Griff moved with her, shifting to keep himself between her and potential threats.

The older man looked up at her approach, his eyes bloodshot and leery.

"Mr. Dunham? I don't know if you remember me. I'm Samantha Ferguson. A friend of Jill's."

He lifted the glass and sipped. Griff could smell the stink of cheap gin.

"The one thought you was smarter'n everybody else. I remember." His words slurred in a way that made Griff wonder if they'd get anything useful out of him.

"I'm looking for Jill. I wondered if maybe you'd seen her recently."

"Why the fuck should I know where she is? Ungrateful bitch hasn't checked on me in months. Off living the high life in Atlanta or wherever the hell." He drained the glass and slapped it down on the table, sneering at Sam. "Never had airs until she started hanging out with you. Maybe you owe me as much as she does."

When he lurched out of his chair, Griff was ready, sliding in front of her to loom over the smaller man. "You don't want to do that." He kept his tone easy and conversational, but he could feel the attention of the other patrons. Hungry, like piranhas waiting to feed on fresh violence. Not if he could help it.

Dunham's breath came hard, and the hands at his sides balled to fists.

Lowering his voice, Griff tried again. "You don't want to take me on again, old man. Didn't end well for you back when."

The man's pale, watery eyes narrowed, studying Griff's face, obviously trying to place him. Hell, he'd been drunk off his ass. Maybe he didn't remember Griff knocking him out cold when he'd caught the man whaling on his daughter back in early high school.

"We asked our question. Now we're gonna go." He reached back for Sam's hand, intent on getting the hell away. Her fingers curled around his. They edged back until they were out of Dunham's reach. Then Griff turned, only to find the path to the door blocked by a regrettably familiar face.

"Well, if it isn't Griff Powell."

Ah, shit. This was why he didn't come home. To avoid the instigators of the worst mistakes from his past. But, of course, Wade Shelton had finished his sentence. The son of a bitch had been a hothead in high school. Griff didn't have any reason to believe that had changed. He needed to keep the situation contained and get Sam out of here safely.

"Wade."

"I hear tell you've parted ways with Uncle Sam. Been working a cushy security job for Kyle Keenan."

Griff said nothing. Wade wasn't looking for confirmation. He was working up to something.

"Tell me, *old buddy*—" The clear emphasis on the term had Griff shifting to the balls of his feet. "—did you give any thought at all to those of us who got sent away?"

Sam's fingers tightened on his. She was the reason he'd been given a choice between military or prison after his arrest. Wade and the rest of them hadn't had anyone like her on their side to lobby with the judge. If not for her, he'd have been put away for being an accessory to armed robbery because he'd driven the getaway car for what was supposed to simply have been shoplifting some beer.

"I don't want any trouble."

Wade laughed. "Y'all hear that? He don't want any trouble!" The false joviality faded. "You weren't thinking of that when you rolled on the rest of us."

Fuck. Was that what he thought had happened? "I didn't roll on anybody."

"Really? You expect me to believe the judge just thought you were special?"

Two other guys edged closer, flanking Wade and effectively cutting off their route of escape.

Griff squeezed Sam's hand, tugging her behind him before letting her go to lift his hands in a placating gesture that gave him plenty of options for neutralizing whatever threat came at him. "I don't know why the judge gave me the option." And he hadn't at the time. Best stick to that. No telling what Wade would do if he knew about Sam's involvement.

Wade took a step closer. "I thought about you walking around all these years while I was in prison. I promised myself I'd give you what you deserved if I ever saw you again."

The bar patrons seemed to hold their collective breath, waiting for the inevitable eruption.

"You really don't want to do that."

"Oh, but I really do." Wade's fist snapped out in an uppercut meant to catch him in the jaw.

Griff dodged and caught the follow up hook, using the momentum to torque Wade's shoulder and drive him to his knees. From the corner of his eye, he saw another of the trio heading for Sam. With brutal efficiency, Griff shoved Wade to the floor and lunged for the would-be assailant, catching him with a throat strike that had him reeling back, crashing into a table. Glass shattered and chairs tumbled over. The third guy looked at his groaning, gasping compatriots and seemed to think better of engaging.

"Smart move." Grabbing Sam, Griff bolted for the door.

Her cheeks were pale, and he could feel her trembling. Everything in him wanted to hold her and offer comfort, but they needed to get the hell out of here before someone followed them outside.

"C'mon. Hurry. In the car." He shut her inside and bolted around to the driver's side.

Neither of them spoke as he peeled out of the parking lot. Griff kept checking the mirrors, looking for a tail, automatically cutting down dimly remembered country roads to confuse anyone who might have decided to come after them. Only when he was satisfied that they were well and truly away did he slow and reach for Sam's hand.

"You okay?"

She still shook. "I... That could have gone really bad."

"Sorry you had to see that. I tried to keep it from coming down to fists."

"No, you were... I've seen you fight before. You were always good. You're better now."

"I'm trained to be."

"I never thought about what might happen if you ran into him again. I guess I just thought he'd be one of those people who spent more time behind bars than not."

"You're likely not wrong. And you're the biggest reason I didn't end up just like him."

Sam looked over at him. "You were never like him. Could never be like him. It's not in you."

She still believed in him? Even after how he'd hurt her? The idea of it humbled him. Her belief always had.

"I'm sorry I put you in that position. I knew it was a long shot that Jill's dad might know anything, and now we're no closer to an answer than we were before. I don't know what else to do."

"We make a report and get the ball rolling with the police."

"The police?"

"Yeah. I should probably clue Xander in to what just happened. Wade threw the first punch, but just in case. We can get him to contact the Atlanta PD. Get them to do a wellness check on Jill. It might be nothing. We hope it is nothing. But it's better to be overcautious."

She was silent for a long moment. "Thank you for helping me with this."

"I've got your back." *Always.*

CHAPTER 7

"Thanks so much for looking into this. I know I'm probably overreacting, but I just can't shake the worry." Sam knotted her hands, concerned they'd crossed a line, stopping by the sheriff's home.

"Better to check and find out everything is fine than to lose time in case it's not. It won't hurt anything to send Atlanta PD out to see what's what."

Xander's wife, Kennedy, perched on the arm of her husband's chair. "Are you sure I can't offer y'all some coffee or tea?"

"Thanks, but no. We've taken up enough of your evening." Griff rose and reached for Sam's hand.

Now that the danger was past, she shouldn't be taking it. It would only confuse things between them. But as he looked down in response to her hesitation, Sam had to acknowledge things were already confused.

She curled her fingers around his, letting him pull her to her feet. Her cheeks prickled with heat as she caught Kennedy's look of speculation. "Sorry for bothering you at home."

Xander rose, too, following them toward the door. "No problem. I'll be in touch to let you know what I find out."

They returned to Sam's car. She didn't even try to go for the driver's seat.

Griff slid behind the wheel. "Well, now what? We've done more or less everything we can do tonight. The tasting is probably over by now."

She winced. "I'm not much keen on going back to the third degree." There'd be questions about what they'd been doing and likely about what was going on between them. She didn't relish any of it.

"All right then. We won't go back yet."

"Where will we go? It's after ten. The sidewalks have already been rolled up."

"I know a place."

He drove back to town, winding through side streets and finally turning onto a narrow dirt road leading into the trees. Partway down, the road dead-ended. Curious, Sam followed when he got out to walk. He turned on the flashlight of his phone as they stepped into the woods.

"I used to come out here when I needed to get away from everybody in high school. Being at Joan's was great, but there was always someone around."

He was bringing her to his secret hideaway? That felt significant. Then again, it felt as if everything with Griff had come to mean something. She understood he would want to talk. That the past had become too huge tonight for her to keep avoiding it. Would she end up with resolution or fresh wounds to the heart she'd tried so hard to protect?

A few minutes later, they emerged from the trees. She realized they were behind the Methodist Church. Griff had never struck her as the religious type.

"I think the sanctuary is locked these days."

"Not the church," he said. "The playground."

"Huh?"

He led her to the side yard, to the little watchtower at the center of the play structure. A slide spiraled down from one side. Monkey bars stuck out from another.

Griff stopped by the ladder. "It's not much, but there's a roof, and it'll keep us mostly out of the wind."

Amused despite herself at the idea of the rebel he'd been hanging out in a church playground to be alone, Sam climbed up. "Gonna be a tight fit. This wasn't built with adults in mind."

"I don't mind if you don't." Griff scrambled through the entrance.

It took a few minutes to situate, trying to accommodate his much longer legs. They wound up shoulder to shoulder, leaning against the one solid wall. She could feel the heat of him through her thin sweater and fought the urge to snuggle closer. Nights were cold this time of year.

For a while they said nothing, listening to the night birds and insects that hadn't yet given up the ghost of autumn. Gradually, some of the tension of the day leeched out. At least until Griff spoke.

"That thing you said earlier in the car…"

"I've said a lot of things today." Many of them probably ill advised.

"That you'll sleep better knowing I'm out of the service."

Shit. Yeah, she hadn't meant to admit to that, but she'd been feeling raw and vulnerable. "What about it?"

"I never thought you'd worry about me."

Flabbergasted, she looked up at him. "I always worried about you. From the day you got shipped off to basic training. You leaving me and going incommunicado didn't change that. No matter how much I may have wanted it to."

He swallowed hard. "I know it's too little, too late, but I'm sorry I hurt you."

Though she tried, Sam couldn't summon the anger she'd kept kindled all these years. Faced with nothing but bone-deep exhaustion, she gave him the truth. "You didn't hurt me, Griffin. I loved you. I married you. Not some fantasy future version of who I thought you could be. *You.* You could have just slept with me. I was more than willing, and you knew it. But instead, you married me. You made promises to me, and you broke them almost immediately. So no, you didn't hurt me. You ripped my heart out over your own insecurities without even considering a conversation or giving me a choice."

Griff bowed his head. "If I'd talked to you, I'd never have been able to go. And I had to go."

"Why?" It was the question she'd tortured herself with for years.

"Because of Jonah."

Whatever she'd expected, none of it had included her brother. "Please don't tell me you left out of some misguided fear that he was going to kick your ass for besmirching my honor or some shit. You did marry me first."

He barked out a laugh. "No. I'm not like your brother. Jonah pursued the Navy and military life because he felt like he had a duty. I thought that would be your yardstick, especially after I found out what you'd said to Judge Mosley to keep me out of jail. I wasn't that guy when we met in Vegas." He sucked in a breath and shifted to face her. "You were the only person in the world who believed in me other than Joan, and I couldn't bear the idea of watching you lose that. I left and re-upped so I could become what you saw. To prove that I'd gone back to serve for the right reasons. So you wouldn't regret me."

Sam sat with that for a bit. She'd always seen

his potential. Always seen who he could be underneath the rough and sometimes brazen behavior. But she finally understood that he'd needed to go back for himself. Because he'd never seen himself that way. It took some of the sting out of what he'd done, because it meant something that he'd wanted to be worthy of her. But that didn't change the fact that he'd broken her heart.

"I would have supported you, you know. If you'd asked. I'd have worried, but I wouldn't have stopped you from going back. We could have made it work."

"Being a military spouse is fucking hard. I didn't want that for you. I wanted to give you the chance at a different life."

Stupid, misguided, well-intentioned man. Sam's throat went thick at the thought of all they'd lost. All they might have been. "I didn't want a different life. I just wanted you." But why would he have believed that back then? Their foundation had been so new, based on memory and shared passion and impulse.

"Samantha." His tone was ripe with regrets.

She'd had enough of those for the night, maybe enough for a lifetime, so she shifted, reaching to frame his face and pull him down to her. She kissed him this time, soft and sweet, wanting so much to convince him he was worthy, even if she didn't know what that meant for her.

His arms came around her, pulling her close. But he made no move to escalate, only held on, as if he needed to drown in this sweetness as much as she did. God, she'd missed the taste of him. The feel of him. She'd just missed *him*.

She was so, so screwed.

Breaking the kiss, she pressed her brow to his. "What are we going to do about this?"

"Explore it."

He'd said that before, in her bedroom. The prospect of it both thrilled and terrified her. A second chance with him could mean everything. Including another opportunity for him to hurt her. Oh, he wouldn't be callous about it.

She understood that. But his personal demons were so deeply rooted, and she wasn't that naive girl anymore who believed she could change him. What if she let him in again, only to be left high and dry the next time his self-doubts got the better of him?

"I need to think about it. Right now, I need to prioritize finding Jill."

Griff pressed a kiss to her brow. "Fair enough. Let's get back to the inn. My ass has gone to sleep."

* * *

DESPITE THE LATE NIGHT, Griff woke per usual at dawn to a regrettably empty bed. He and Sam had successfully avoided everyone when they came in. He'd left her at her door, not pushing his luck for another kiss, though every cell in his body had wanted to take her mouth, knowing he could tip her past good sense into lust. Lust would only solve one of their problems.

I didn't want a different life. I wanted you.

Her words had stayed with him long into the night, following him into sleep, where he'd dreamed of the life they could've had, if only he'd been braver. Coming home to her at the end of deployment. Fixing up a house into the home he'd never had. Cuddling on the sofa with a cheerful mutt sprawled at their feet. Standing over a crib, watching their child sleep.

Christ, that had gotten him. He'd never really thought of having kids. That was for other people. More stable people, who didn't come from the kind of fucked up background he did. Then again, his foster siblings were proving left and right that origins weren't everything. They were carrying on the legacy of love Joan had instilled in all of them.

Could he?

Yeah. With Sam, he thought he could have all of it. And he'd reached a place where he believed he deserved a shot at it. But she'd have to get on board with picking up where they'd left off.

She wanted to think, so he'd give her the space to do that. At least he felt confident that she *would* think about it now. She hadn't told him to go to hell, and given how he'd hurt her, she'd have been justified. Trust would take time to rebuild. At the very least, he owed her that.

So how was he going to go about it? This bachelor-bachelorette weekend thing was over today. Sure, they'd see each other again for the wedding in a few weeks, but he wasn't ready to just let her go. Giving her space to think didn't mean keeping himself out of sight, out of her normal life. She needed to see that he intended to stick this time.

Shit. Was it time to think about moving? Or rather, settling somewhere? Since he'd separated from the Marines earlier this year, he'd been on the road for several months doing close personal protection for Kyle, and since the tour wrapped, had bounced around from one temporary situation to the next, staying on call for when Kyle needed him, but otherwise reconnecting with his other brothers. Maybe he'd been waiting for exactly this. A chance again with Sam.

The phone on the nightstand rang. Griff grabbed it and flipped it open. "Powell."

"Hey Griff, it's Xander."

Griff sat up. "You've got news?"

"Such as it is."

Tensing, he rolled out of bed. "Hang on, I'll get Sam."

Pulling open his door, he crossed the hall, knocking softly on hers. After a few seconds, he heard the sound of movement. The door swung open to a heavy-eyed Samantha in plaid pajama pants and one of the little camisoles that drove him crazy. No power on earth could've kept him from noticing her breasts in that. His body stirred.

She rubbed at her eyes and yawned. "Griff, what are you—"

He pushed past her.

"—doing here?"

"Xander's on the phone."

That wiped the sleep right off her face. She

shut the door and crossed her arms in a self-protective stance as Griff put the phone on speaker. "Okay, go ahead."

"Sorry to call so early, but I just heard back from Atlanta PD. They did a drive-by of Jill's apartment. Knocked on the door. No one was home, and her car wasn't there. No sign of anything worrisome."

Sam's brows drew together. "So that's… it?"

"Unless somebody finds evidence of foul-play that would spark a more thorough investigation. Right now, no news is good news. In all actuality, most folks will turn up within a few days. She'll probably be back to work bright and early tomorrow morning with stories to tell about her crazy weekend."

"I see." Sam's tone clearly said she didn't.

"Thanks for checking, Xander."

"Sure thing. If there's anything else I can do, don't hesitate to reach out."

"We appreciate it." Griff hung up. "Well, that's another thing crossed off the list."

"Another dead end, you mean."

"As Xander said, it's probably fine."

"But is it? Or is that just a thing everybody keeps saying to placate me? My gut says something's wrong."

He dropped his phone onto the dresser and closed the short distance between them, stroking his hands down her bare arms and trying not to think about the last time they'd been this close to undressed together. "I'm not a man who dismisses gut feelings. They've kept me alive on more than one occasion. Let's just get through this last brunch thing, and we'll figure out what to do next."

Sam nodded, her gaze finally focusing on him. Or, more properly, his bare chest. He realized he'd walked across the hall in nothing but a pair of sweatpants. She blinked, those big dark eyes dilating as they fixed on the tattoo over his heart. Her tongue darted out to moisten lips gone suddenly rosy.

"You should... get dressed." The strain in her voice said she wished he'd do anything but.

Or maybe that was the straining he was trying to ignore in his pants. "You, too."

Neither of them moved.

One easy motion would tumble her onto the bed, into the mussed covers. A few strategic tugs, and he could have his mouth on her again, tasting those nipples that had tightened to stiff peaks behind the flimsy cotton of her cami top, feasting on the heat between her thighs.

"Don't look at me like that," she whispered.

"Like what?"

"Like you're reliving our entire wedding night in your head right now."

"I've added a whole lot of fantasies to that one," he growled.

"Griffin, please..."

It was the please that did him in. Because it wasn't the please he wanted. He wouldn't cross that line until she asked him to. No matter how much it killed him.

Digging for some shred of control, he released her and stepped back. "I'll see you downstairs at breakfast."

Yanking open the door, he stepped into the hall just as Ari stepped out of the bathroom with an armful of towels. She looked at him, at the room he was stepping out of and his general state of undress and arousal, and obviously drew some conclusions. Her smile spread slow and delighted. She dropped the towels into a basket at her feet and gave him a double thumbs up.

Fucking perfect.

Saying nothing, he went back to his own room.

If he lingered longer than necessary, well, he was only human. He wasn't a brunch kind of guy to begin with, and, in all likelihood, this one would come with a side of interrogation. Pass. But eventually, he manned up and headed downstairs. His appearance was greeted with smirks from the men and speculation from the women.

"Late night?" Mick tried and failed to keep a straight face.

Griff grunted and made a beeline for the

coffeepot at the end of the buffet. No reason to dignify that with a response when there were Belgian waffles, eggs Benedict, and a boatload of other breakfast goodies that made his stomach growl. Damn, but Athena could cook.

"Where did you two go last night?" Erin asked.

"To see Jill's dad."

That wiped amusement off everyone's faces. Spotting Sam in the doorway, he turned to pour another cup, adding the cream and one sugar she liked.

"Isn't he out… you know?" Mariko asked in a hushed tone, as if verbalizing the name of the place was akin to speaking of Voldemort.

"The holler. Yeah. Hence Griff's bodyguard detail." Sam accepted the coffee with a nod of thanks, folding her hands around the mug and closing her eyes as she inhaled.

She'd swapped the pajamas for jeans and a soft cotton shirt under one of the wrap sweaters she liked. The look was very girl-next-door and almost as appealing as the sleepwear.

"Did you find out anything?" Kendrick asked.

Griff pulled his attention away from his ex-wife. "Nothing useful. He hasn't seen Jill in months."

Cressida breezed in, apparently dressed for brunch at a country club, complete with pearls and a cloud of some expensive-smelling perfume. "Oh my God, are y'all still on about this?"

Sam stiffened. "Some of us actually give a damn about the welfare of our friends."

"Y'all are a bunch of worrywarts. I found an email from her in my spam folder this morning."

"What? When? What did she say?"

Cressida made a big production out of pouring a glass of orange juice. "That she wasn't going to be able to make it. She had to be in Gatlinburg to perform for some festival, but she'll definitely make it for the wedding. So see? She's fine. She just flaked out. Exactly like I said."

Erin sighed in relief. "Oh, good. I knew

there had to be a logical explanation."

Kendrick laid his arm across the back of his bride-to-be's chair. "Glad that mystery is solved."

The answer clearly didn't sit well with Sam. "But that doesn't make sense. Why would she email you and then not respond to a single one of my messages?"

"I'm the matron of honor. I organized this weekend, in case you forgot." In typical Cressida style, she managed to look down her nose without even angling her face. "As for the rest, maybe you aren't as good a friend as you thought."

Erin groaned. "For the love of God, Cressida, give it a rest. I'm not going to have any of this sniping at my wedding. Hear me?"

"I'm just stating facts."

Griff could practically hear Sam grinding her teeth and ranged himself between them. "Ignore her. Meanwhile, try to eat something. You barely touched dinner last night. You don't want to offend the chef."

As he'd wanted, the reference to his notoriously temperamental sister got the flutter of a smile. She added a waffle and some bacon to her plate and grabbed a seat. He called it a win that she left room for him beside her. The lack of avoidance did not go unnoticed by his brothers. Declan's eyebrows were practically doing an interpretive dance trying to communicate... something. Griff definitely hadn't had enough coffee to translate that.

Everyone clearly considered the subject of Jill's absence closed, and conversation turned to the wedding. But Sam stayed quiet, obviously not satisfied with the lack of definitive answers.

When talk turned to packing and getting on the road, she slipped out to the back porch. No longer concerned with what the rest of them thought, Griff trailed her outside. He found her staring out at the mountains, another mug of coffee clutched between her hands.

"You're not convinced."

"I know it's probably stupid. But I just can't shake the idea that something is wrong."

He nodded and sipped at his own coffee. "When do we leave?"

"What?"

"For Gatlinburg. You want to go check it out, don't you?"

She stared at him. "I'm due back tomorrow in Chattanooga. I have classes to teach."

"Are you going to be able to concentrate on those until you have actual answers?"

"Probably not," she conceded. "I suppose I could send their assignments online. But what does that have to do with 'we'? You surely have your own life to get back to this week."

"There is nothing I have on my plate that's more important than you." It was the simple, unvarnished truth.

A swirl of emotion swam into her eyes. Gratitude. Worry. She didn't know yet if she could believe him. But he'd show her. He'd show her every single day until she couldn't see anything else.

"Go pack your bags and email your students, Professor. We're going sleuthing."

CHAPTER 8

"Have you seen this woman?" Sam held out her phone for the millionth time to show the picture of Jill she'd nabbed from social media.

The fifty-something venue manager slipped on her glasses and briefly studied the image. "Nope. I'm sorry."

"Are you sure? She would have been with one of the bands."

"Honey, there were literally more than a hundred bands here for the festival this weekend. And that was on top of the tourists. You're looking for a needle in a haystack."

Sam wilted. "Thank you for your time." The manager walked away, and she rejoined Griff at the front doors. "Any luck?"

But she knew the answer before he even opened his mouth. They'd combed Gatlinburg, hitting up every venue they could find, checking with every hotel, motel, and lodging along the way. No one had recognized Jill's photo or her name. Sam's feet and head ached, and she was starting to feel foolish as well as discouraged.

"We're taking a break." Griff punctuated the pronouncement by taking her arm and propelling her into motion.

"But we still have a little less than half the list to get through." She had no idea how they were going to pull that off. It was already after dark.

"You're dead on your feet. We're getting food and regrouping."

She didn't have the energy to argue, and honestly, it was nice to have someone else make a decision. All her brainpower had been going toward considering the angles, trying to think of some other means of finding her friend. So far, all she'd learned was that she definitely had no business quitting her day job to be a private detective.

Griff steered her into the first restaurant they came to that didn't have a line trailing out the door. A few minutes later, they were seated at a tiny table in the back.

"Your server will be with you in a minute."

As the hostess strode away, Sam groaned. "I shouldn't have sat down. I'm not sure how I'm going to get moving again." Without momentum to keep her going, all the exhaustion she'd ignored crashed down on her like a rockslide. Everything hurt.

"You'll be better after getting some food in you."

"Maybe." She rubbed at the throbbing in her temples. "I thought this would be easier. It's been so long since I've been down here that I forgot how much they have crammed in such a small area. And there's more now than there was before. We might be able to hit up all the formal venues, but I didn't think about the free-standing stages they set up just for the festival. And there's no way we can manage every possible place to stay. Not with all the AirBnBs and rental cabins. We could do this for a week and still not find a damned thing."

Griff didn't appear phased. Or tired. She hated him a little bit for that, but after twelve years in the Marines, of course, he was in better physical shape than she was.

"It only takes one person to give us a new lead."

True enough. And yet... "I'm starting to think we have a better shot at winning the lottery."

"Hi, there. I'm Jessie, and I'll be your server tonight. What can I get y'all to drink?"

Griff shot her an easy smile. "Sweet tea. And can I ask you something, Jessie?"

The girl blinked and flushed. "Of course."

He snagged the phone Sam had laid down on the edge of the table and flashed the picture of Jill on the lock screen. "We're looking for a friend of ours who was performing at the festival this weekend. You didn't happen to see her, did you?"

"She doesn't look familiar, but we've been jumping this weekend. I can ask around to the other servers, though."

Brightening a little at the kindness, Sam straightened. "That would be great." Jessie snapped a picture with her own phone and disappeared to retrieve their drink orders.

Griff braced his elbows on the table. "Okay, let's discuss next steps. We're running low on time tonight, so we'll probably want to prioritize the remaining venues on the list, as they'll be closing and probably won't reopen until later in the day tomorrow."

"It's as good a plan as any," Sam conceded. "But what if we don't find anything? What if we've wasted all this time and effort?"

"I don't consider any time with you a waste.

But in terms of our investigation, we could head to Atlanta next and see if we can find any clues to her whereabouts. The cops don't have reason to canvas her neighborhood, but we can."

Sam stared at him. "You'd do that?"

"I'm sticking, Samantha. For whatever you need. You're worried, and by now, so am I. Because I know as well as you do that all the reasons Jill was considered flaky in high school had nothing to do with her being a flake and everything to do with being the only child of a single, alcoholic father. I sure as hell hope she calls you back tomorrow, and we find out we've been worried over nothing, but if she doesn't, if something really has happened to her, who else is going to look for her?"

Warmth and gratitude flooded through her that he was taking this seriously and not just humoring her. It was more proof that she hadn't been wrong all those years ago. That he was still the guy who showed up when it mattered.

She curled her fingers around his. "Thank you."

Jessie came back with their tea. "I asked everyone else on shift. No one remembers seeing your friend. But someone suggested you could make a post on the festival's social media pages to ask more broadly if anyone has seen her."

"Oh, that's a great idea. Thank you!"

They gave their orders, and Sam immediately opened her phone to make the post. "Done. That'll be a smarter, not harder move for sure." Catching Griff's pensive expression, she sat back. "What?"

"I've just been thinking. We came here based on questionable intel."

"What do you mean?"

"We didn't see the email. If the news had come from Erin, I wouldn't blink, but—"

"But Cressida hates me," she finished. "You think she made it all up to send me on a wild goose chase?"

He leaned back with a shrug. "That might be

assuming a whole lot more forethought than Cressida is likely to give. I don't know if she expected you to actually go looking. She might've said it just to shut you up. She got pissed all weekend every time you brought up that there might be an actual problem that might've pulled everybody's focus away from the event she'd planned. But, hell, I didn't know about at least half the shit she pulled on you in high school, so at this point, I wouldn't put it past her to try to manipulate you into running around like a chicken with your head cut off."

Wasn't that a comforting thought? "So what are you saying?"

"Maybe before we go to Atlanta, we talk to Cressida first. See if we can get any more information on this alleged email."

Sam considered. Getting more information, taking a little more time to think was the smart play. So far, everything she'd done had been reactive. Surely, proactive was better?

"I doubt she'll talk to me."

One corner of his mouth turned up in that

way that had always promised mischief. "Hard to ignore you if we show up on her doorstep."

"Really? You think we should drive down to Mississippi to confront her?"

"I'm just saying it's an option. And if we confront her in person, she won't expect it and has less time to cook up a cover story. Let's be real—it's not the craziest thing we've ever done."

"It's a fair point." It would be hard to top their weekend in Vegas on that front. "It's definitely worth considering. For now, let's finish what we've started here. We can make that call tomorrow."

"Agreed. Speaking of which, we need to secure actual lodging for the night."

Jessie slid their plates in front of them. "Oh, good luck with that. There's a huge accountant's conference starting tomorrow that's taking up most of the rooms in town. Everybody came in this afternoon."

Sam waved that away. "I'm sure we'll find something,"

* * *

"CAN I HELP YOU?" The front desk clerk barely took his eyes off the TV quietly playing *Friends* reruns in the corner.

"Two things," Griff said, leaning on the counter. "First, have you seen this woman?" He held out the printed picture of Jill, waiting until the guy finally focused.

"Never seen her before." His attention swung back to the TV, rapt, as if he'd never seen the turkey episode before.

They'd gotten the same answer everywhere else, so Griff hadn't really expected anything else, but he'd had to ask. "Okay, two, do you have any rooms available?"

God, Griff hoped so, or they might be sleeping in the car. This was the fifteenth—seventeenth?—place they'd tried. Sam was about to drop, and he didn't want to drive up through Pigeon Forge on to Sevierville, only to get more of the same.

With a sigh, the clerk rolled his eyes and

dragged his attention to the computer. How dare they expect him to do his job? Griff held in his irritation as fingers began clattering over the keyboard.

"Got one. Had a cancellation a couple hours ago."

"We'll take it." They hadn't discussed sharing a room, but the night had made it clear that beggars couldn't be choosers.

Sam didn't even blink. But that might've been because she'd fallen asleep with her eyes open. Her posture was slumped, and she swayed a little as Griff dug out his wallet. She still hadn't moved or spoken by the time he'd gotten the key.

He tucked an arm around her shoulders. "C'mon, baby. Let's get you off your feet."

She put one foot in front of the other, docile as a lamb. That, more than anything else, proved how exhausted she was. He led her out the door and down the cracked sidewalk to the room they'd been assigned. It was hard not to think about the last time they'd shared a room.

A luxury resort hotel this was not, but his sense of tension was the same as he swung open the door to see the lone, king-size bed.

Sam roused enough to blink at it. "Oh."

"I'll sleep on the floor." The offer was automatic. The same one he'd made all those years ago, before he'd known the taste of her, the feel and shape of her beneath his hands. He'd been attempting to be the gentleman she deserved. Now, though, it felt like the barest form of self-preservation.

"Don't be ridiculous. There's no telling what's on the carpet in this place."

He'd definitely slept under worse conditions in the field. "There aren't enough pillows for a wall." That had been her answer to his discomfort in Vegas. As if a barricade of feathers and fabric was enough to stop him from thinking about her sleeping within arm's reach in nothing but sleep shorts and one of those tank tops designed to torture a man.

She mustered up a smirk. "We're grownups. I think we can handle it."

Speak for yourself.

Wandering over to the window, she turned on the room heater. With an asthmatic wheeze, it began to blow.

"I'll go grab our stuff."

If he took a little longer than necessary to move the car and collect their bags, well, he needed a little pep talk to prepare himself for platonically sharing a bed with the woman he wanted to ravish.

When he set down their bags, she still stood by the window unit, hands tucked beneath her arms. "Hopefully this thing will kick in soon."

Platonically sharing a bed and possibly body heat? Is the universe trying to kill me? But Griff only handed over her suitcase.

She set it on the desk, pulling out the neatly organized toiletry kit and pajamas and jerking a thumb toward the bathroom. "Mind if I get in there first?"

"Be my guest."

He locked up and quickly changed into sweatpants and a T-shirt as he heard the rush of running water and an electric toothbrush behind the thin door. A few minutes later, she came back out in the flannel pants and cami top she'd been wearing this morning. God, had that *really* been today? It felt like a week ago.

Griff kept his gaze on her face, noting the strain and worry there, underlying the exhaustion. "Get some rest, Professor. I won't be long."

She was in bed when he came back out from brushing his teeth, a still form beneath the thin coverlet. Moving quietly so as not to wake her, he switched off the light and made his way to the other side. Bed springs squeaked as he eased his weight onto the mattress.

"Griff?" Her voice was a quiet rasp over the faint hum of the heater.

"I thought you were asleep."

"I feel like I should be. I'm tired enough."

"But?"

"My brain won't turn off. And the covers aren't heavy enough."

He'd promised himself he wouldn't touch her. But this wasn't about seduction. She needed comfort and contact. He could give her that without pushing for more. Reaching out in the dark, he gathered her up, tucking her against his chest. He'd thought she might protest, put distance back between them. Instead, she nestled her head against his shoulder, cuddling closer, as if it had been hours instead of years since they'd lain together like this. That had to mean something, right? She had to be softening to the idea of giving him another chance.

"I forgot how much of a human heater you are."

Smiling to himself, he pressed a soft kiss to her brow. "I've got your back."

She sighed at that and relaxed another few degrees.

Griff settled back against the pillow. "Get some sleep."

A little—or maybe a long while later, her body finally relaxed into sleep. She felt exactly right like this, snuggled close to his side, her legs tangled with his, her breath a gentle stir against his throat. Much as he wanted her, he wanted this, too. The trust. The contentment. He'd missed out on this before with his panicked exit from her life, and he'd robbed them both of this comfort.

He'd give it to her every night from now on, if she'd let him. He'd give her everything. He just had to convince her to take it.

CHAPTER 9

*S*am floated in a warm, comfortable haze, caught somewhere between waking and dreams. There were reasons to get up, get going, but she couldn't remember them at the moment. All she wanted was to stay in this fantasy that she wasn't alone, that it wasn't a body pillow she was wrapped around, and it wasn't the sheets she clutched in her hand. Her heart didn't hurt here, and that rare state of affairs deserved to be savored.

The pillow moved. Just a subtle shift against

her torso and a pressure behind her shoulders, as if she were being held.

Pillows did not have arms.

Rising closer to consciousness, she registered the legs twined with hers and the big hand curved over her shoulder, a warm weight against her tattoo. Turning her head into the chest that she'd been using as a pillow, she inhaled the scent of sleep-warmed skin. Delicious, intoxicating comfort.

Griffin.

She knew the smell of him, remembered it, though their time together had been fleeting and so very long ago.

He was still here.

Okay, maybe that was because she was wrapped around him like a vine, her hand fisting his t-shirt like a security blanket. But he held on to her just as tight.

He held on.

There was no reason for him to have slipped out in the dead of night. But she hadn't thought he'd had a reason before, and she'd still woken alone. She hadn't really realized she'd expected the same this morning. His solid, steady presence had her bruised and battered heart thudding hard against her ribs.

He'd been saying for days he wanted to try again. That he wouldn't repeat his mistakes from the past. Wouldn't hurt her again. Perhaps nothing he could have said or done would have made her believe it more than this right here. It was a foolish metric. One night could hardly make up for the loss of years.

But beyond that, he was here, on this improbable, likely ridiculous search for a friend. He hadn't belittled her concern, hadn't pointed out all the irrationality of some of her actions. He'd simply continued to show up because she needed it. It was what he'd done for most of their friendship. What he'd done in Vegas, before he'd blown things all to hell. At what point did the lion's share of his behavior outweigh that one hurtful act? The foolishly romantic heart she'd been pretending not to have any-more wanted to let him in again, and she was so, so tired of fighting it.

Griff shifted to press a kiss to her brow, much as he'd done last night. Contentment slid through her at the soft brush of his lips, and she sighed, relaxing utterly boneless against him. He kissed her again, as if he couldn't help himself. Soothed by the contact and wanting more, she tipped her head back and back, so he could keep trailing kisses along her temple, across her cheek. Each featherlike brush of his lips lit sweet sparks of sensation, until he reached her mouth, and the sweetness spawned something more.

She sank into the kiss, drowning in the flavor of him. In the taste of tenderness and apology. Yearning built as memory and reality collided. He was here. At last, he was really here. With her. Was she really going to deny herself what she'd wanted all this time? She loved him. Her powers of self-delusion weren't strong enough to combat the truth of that, and she couldn't hold herself apart any longer.

Untangling her leg, she rolled to straddle him, diving deeper into the kiss as she settled her weight against the bulge of his morning wood. A groan escaped them both at the contact. It was too much and not nearly enough. Seeking relief, she began to rock. His hands curled around her hips, holding her closer as he bucked against her in short, shallow thrusts. Pleasure ribboned through her like smoke from a fire she desperately wanted to chase.

"Samantha." His voice was gravel against her lips, but she heard the question. The concern. He wouldn't press this because she'd asked him not to.

So she answered in the clearest way she could, stripping off her shirt and bending to him again. "Need you."

That was all the directive he needed.

He rolled them, yanking off his t-shirt with one hand before lowering his head to take her breast. Sensation exploded through her.

"Oh, God." She stroked her hands down the muscled planes of his back as his busy, talented mouth suckled her nipples. She needed skin, needed to feel him everywhere.

Clearly on the same page, his fingers hooked in the waistband of her pajama bottoms and underwear, dragging them down. He had to abandon her breasts to get them off, and she whimpered in protest when he didn't immediately come back.

But he only growled, "Need you," and fixed his mouth between her thighs.

On a cry, she dove her fingers into his hair as he feasted, licking and sucking, feverishly drawing out every drop of pleasure until she flew, sobbing out his name. He'd always been able to wreck her, and still she wanted more. Wanted all.

Quaking, she reached for him as he crawled up her body, looming over her. The weight of him in the cradle of her hips was achingly familiar and so very right. She slid her fingers into the hair at his nape and wrapped around him, welcoming him into her body with joy. They both shuddered as he filled her, sinking slowly into her wet heat, until all the years and distance were gone. Those glorious, gorgeous eyes bore into hers, almost black with his arousal, as he pulled back and thrust in again. She felt seen and possessed. More, she felt cherished as they moved in sync, on a wordless surge of rising pleasure. And as she quickened around him, felt the answering pulse of his body, the last of her defenses crumbled.

GRIFF AVOIDED CRUSHING SAM... barely. The elbows he'd braced on either side of her took the brunt of his weight. But he could still feel the press of her breasts against his chest as they panted. God, he loved those breasts. He wanted to worship them some more. He wanted to worship all of her some more, to make up for lost time and fill in all those fantasies he'd conjured in the last eight years. There were a hell of a lot of them.

He'd get to it in a little while, when he could move again. In a month or two. Right now, he just wanted to bask because there was no better way to start the day. Heaven was right here, skin-to-skin with this woman, nothing between them. No more secrets. No more distance. No—

His eyes popped open in dawning realization. *Oh God.*

Sam's hands stroked lazy patterns on his shoulders. Her face was relaxed, content, her lips curved in the same feline smile he'd delighted in wringing from her on their wedding night. And he was about to ruin all of it.

"Samantha," he croaked.

Without opening her eyes, she hummed a noise of question.

Griff swallowed, wishing he didn't have to make this confession. "I forgot to use a condom."

He waited for the sharp intake of breath. The oh shit panic.

Her eyes fluttered open and focused on his. No alarm. No rising horror. The body beneath his stayed languid, but for the aftershocks that still squeezed his dick.

Jesus, he should pull out, no matter how amazing it felt.

But when he made to do just that, she locked her legs around him. "You're clean, yes?"

"Yeah, but..."

"The horse is already out of the barn on the rest, and nothing on earth has ever felt as good as having you inside me." She considered. "Except the last time you were here. I want to enjoy it."

He couldn't even feel smug about the compliment or the fact that he was a thousand percent on the same page. The situation wasn't that simple. Nothing between them ever was, and he absolutely did not want to screw this up by not considering the consequences.

Stroking damp strands of hair away from

her face, he murmured, "What if you get pregnant?"

Her touch remained languid, her voice soft and conversational. "Does the idea of that scare you?"

No. It didn't scare him at all. In fact, the idea of her carrying his baby had him going hard again. Because apparently he was a Neanderthal.

But didn't it scare *her*?

Her eyes went impossibly darker, and she arched against him. "I think you like the idea. Or part of you does, at least."

Griff struggled to hold still and not swallow his tongue as she squeezed him with her inner muscles. "Yeah, I do. God that feels good."

She did it again, and he nearly choked.

"Just... stop for a minute. I'm trying to say something important here, and you're draining all the blood from my brain."

Her mouth quirked. "Sorry." But she didn't actually look repentant.

Griff drew in a long breath. Then another,

trying to find some control and the words he needed her to hear. "Look, I want everything with you. Marriage. Family. A life. The life I ran away from before. But I don't want you to ever think I'd try to trap you like that. You asked for time, and I intended to give it to you. I want you to want to be with me because you want it. Not because of an obligation."

The amusement faded from her expression. She reached up, framing his face. "I have never been with you out of obligation. Not before and not now. It was always because I love you."

Love. Present tense.

Griff's breath backed up in his lungs, and he couldn't speak. He'd waited so damned long, hoped so damned much that he could win her back, earn the love he hadn't protected the way he should have.

Her gaze searched his face. "I hope you understand that I wouldn't take this risk with you if I didn't."

She wouldn't. He knew that. That she'd risk this with him meant on some level she wanted it. Wanted him for longer than the moment, longer than their mission. And yet…

"A risk isn't the same thing as a choice. Do you want kids?"

Were they seriously having this conversation right now? When they'd barely come back together?

She stayed quiet for a long time. So long, he wondered if she was afraid to answer.

The confession came in a whisper. "There was a part of me that was disappointed I wasn't pregnant after you left." Her mouth twisted in a wry smile. "It would've been terrible timing all around. Would've made things a lot harder. But I would have had a piece of you. A piece of us."

The idea of it rocked him. "Samantha."

"And then I was relieved. Because if I'd had a child, I'd have told you, and you'd have come back, and… I didn't want to trap you, either."

He dropped his brow to hers. "Being with you could never be a cage."

She slid her hand up to his nape, fingering

the ends of his hair. "Do you remember what I told you about risk all those years ago?"

He thought back. They'd been discussing gambling and his absolute distaste for it, given his father's addiction. "You said something to the effect that there's nothing inherently wrong with it, so long as you know the parameters going in. That calculated risk wasn't reckless."

"You were always my calculated risk." She brushed her lips over his. "And my heart always knew you'd be worth it."

Nothing and no one had ever wrecked him as much as this woman. "I love you so fucking much."

"Then make love to me again. Like this."

Deliberately bare. Knowing they could be starting a life. God, he wanted that. Wanted it more than his next breath. This was so much more than the second chance he'd been hoping for. This was everything.

If a part of him wondered if it was too soon, if this was yet another reckless impulse, it was drowned out by the hot, silken grip of her body as he began to move. His eyes stayed on hers, drinking in every flicker of pleasure, adjusting his pace, his thrusts to draw it out. Slow, so achingly slow. As if they had endless hours to bask in the heat.

"Griffin. Deeper."

Hooking one of her legs over his shoulder, he pressed in again, sinking in to the hilt.

"Oh God, yes, there." The rough strain in her voice told him he was on the right track.

The slow, inexorable rise began. Each long thrust and retreat dragged against her clit, delicious and perfect friction. Sweat slicked his skin, and he trembled with the effort to hold on, steeping her in as much sensation as possible. Wanting to wipe out the memory of the pain he'd caused her with pleasure.

Her whimpers gave way to moans, breath going ragged. "So good. I love feeling you like this." She shuddered, close. So close.

"What do you need?"

Those deep, dark eyes fixed on his. "You. All of you." She emphasized the order by clamping down, holding him deep, and he could do nothing but obey.

Lightning erupted down his spine until he was coming and coming, emptying everything he was into everything he hoped they'd be.

CHAPTER 10

The drive to Mississippi should have been awkward as hell. Four hundred fifty miles for her rational brain to kick back in. Seven and a half hours to think about all the ramifications of this morning. It was crazy. Crazier even than marrying him in the first place, and she didn't have the excuse of falling under some romantic spell. She'd made a very deliberate choice to make love with Griff without protection, knowing a baby could be a consequence. His baby. A piece of the man she'd loved for half her life.

God, the idea of that shouldn't turn her on so damned much. Not with things so new and unsettled between them. They shouldn't be leaping without discussing the future—again. But here they were. Something about him always made her want to jump. Because deep down, she'd always believed he'd catch her. That belief had bitten her in the ass before, but he wouldn't leave her again. She'd felt how much he wanted this. Wanted her.

If a tiny voice reminded her that wanting had never been their problem, she ignored it. She wanted to cling to the joy of being with him again. To glory in the freedom of letting her romantic heart breathe and dream again. The rest could wait for a little while. Their search for Jill had taken on the same liminal, time-out-of-time feeling as that long ago weekend in Vegas, and as then, she didn't want to break the spell by diving too soon into the practicalities of real life. A mistake? Maybe. But she'd meant what she'd told him. He'd always been her calculated risk.

The same couldn't be said of this plan to show up on Cressida's doorstep. It felt foolhardy. If she'd lied or withheld information, why would she admit to any of that now?

"You're thinking awfully hard over there, Professor."

"Just wondering if we've come all this way on a fool's errand. She's not likely to help us."

"Maybe not. But knowing whether she's lying is still useful information. Either way, we're nearly there."

The GPS led them into an affluent section of Oxford. Stately homes sat on large, well-groomed lots that spoke of yard services and housekeepers. Everything about this place was a show of wealth and status. The single-story brick house, with plantation-style columns across a wide veranda, was no different.

"Well, I guess the surgeon she married is keeping her in the lifestyle she always felt like she deserved."

Griff merely grunted and parked at the curb.

This place was about as far from where he'd come from as it was possible to get. Did that bother him on some level?

"How do we want to handle this? We don't even know if she's home."

"Then we start there." He shoved out of the car.

On their way up the walk, Sam resisted the urge to take his hand. Much as she wanted the connection, greeting Cressida while marking her territory was hardly going to get things off on the right foot. Not that she really thought there was a right way to approach this.

Griff rang the bell. As they waited, Sam checked her watch. It wasn't quite five. Did Cressida have a job? She hadn't mentioned work over the weekend, but Sam had spent the whole time trying to avoid her.

The door opened. Cressida stood in the pristine entryway looking ready for a country club photoshoot. Her eyes widened the at the sight of Griff, her mouth curving into a flirtatious smile. "What an unexpected surprise."

"No." The single syllable was curt, cold, shutting down any expectation that he'd play her game.

Okay. No good cop, bad cop. "May we come in?"

Only then did Cressida notice Sam. Her mouth dropped open, her perfectly tweezed blonde brows puckering. "What are you doing here?"

"Hoping to have a conversation. It won't take long."

Cressida hesitated, clearly weighing her options. Curiosity won out. She stepped back so they could enter.

Into the lion's den.

Griff pressed a hand to the small of Sam's back and nudged her forward. The move wasn't lost on their reluctant host. Her eyes narrowed, assessing what it meant. Sam was small enough, petty enough, that she hoped Cressida could read in their body language that they were lovers. Let her be the one stewing for once.

The foyer opened to an *Architectural-Digest-*

worthy living room in eye-popping white. The kind of room no one would be comfortable sitting in, let alone living in. But Rebecca Ferguson had drilled manners deep. "You have a lovely home."

The observation of social niceties seemed to throw Cressida off, triggering her own etiquette. "Thank you. Can I offer you something to drink?"

"Water would be great, thank you."

Trapped by her own social script, she turned and headed further into the house. Without waiting for an invitation, Sam followed her back to the kitchen, feeling Griff prowling on her heels. The space was another magazine spread, full of more white and gleaming stainless appliances. The pots hanging on the rack above the counter didn't even look used. Were they pod people? Robots? Was this a movie set?

Cressida filled a glass and handed it over. "Griff?" When he just shook his head, she seemed to run out of good hostess energy. "What is this about?"

Sam took point. "I want a copy of the email from Jill."

"Excuse me?" Ah, there was the standard disdain.

"We just went all over Gatlinburg, questioning people, looking for anyone who might have seen her. Didn't find a single one. So, on the off chance that you misread or accidentally left out something in your report, I want to see the email." Not that she believed for a moment any omissions had been accidental, but there was no reason to start off with accusations.

Cressida's gaze swung to Griff. "You went with her for this wild goose chase?"

He folded his arms, squaring those big shoulders until he loomed, even from ten feet away. "Is that an admission you sent us on one and there is no email?"

"I had no way of knowing y'all would go haring off to play private detective. And even if I had, why would I do that?"

"I don't know why the fuck you do anything. But it seemed like the kind of spiteful, malicious shit you'd throw at Sam." Temper simmered just under the surface, and if she didn't do something, he was going to go off.

"Griff." Sam laid a hand on his arm and found corded steel. "Not helping." Squeezing in warning, she kept her own tone placid. "Look, I know we've never gotten on. I'm not here looking for some kumbaya moment with you. The fact is, right now, you are the last person we know of who had any contact with Jill. So please, give us a copy of the email."

At last, seeming to accept the idea that something more might be going on, Cressida dropped her combative posture. "You still haven't heard from her?"

"No. Neither has anyone else."

"I don't know if my spam folder has emptied or not, but I'll see what I can do." She left them alone in the kitchen.

Sam stroked a hand across Griff's rock-hard shoulders, hoping to soothe. "Stand down, Marine."

His jaw worked. "There are so many things I want to say to her."

"Water under the bridge. There's no point. And in this we need her, so play nice."

She took his growl as assent and stepped away, retrieving her water. Throat parched from all the recirculated air in the car, she drained the glass and strode over to the fridge to refill it. The appointment card on the counter seemed so out of place in the ruthless neatness, she automatically scanned it, along with the labels on the small row of pill bottles lined up like soldiers against the back of the counter. Absorbing the implications, she turned away, feeling like a voyeur.

Cressida came back, a sheet of paper in her hand. "This is it."

Sam read the email.

To: Cressida Milton <cmilton@mailnet.com>

From: Jill Dunham <jill.dunham13@south-mail.com>

Re: Bachelorette Weekend

Dear Cressida,

Please tell Erin I'm sorry for missing this weekend. I've landed an opportunity I can't turn down to sub for a major band at the festival in Gatlinburg this weekend. If it works out, I'll be joining them on the next leg of their tour. But nothing on earth can keep me away from the wedding!

Jill

So she hadn't lied about Gatlinburg. Sam passed the email to Griff.

Cressida crossed her arms. "It sounds like maybe it worked out for her."

"Or like she got played," he muttered.

Sam felt the blood drain out of her cheeks.

Griff winced. "Sorry. Naturally paranoid."

"But Jill's not. This is something she's wanted forever. What if she did get played? What if somebody used this to kidnap her?"

Griff took her by the shoulders and shifted her to face him. "Breathe and stop catastrophizing, Professor. That's a lot of what ifs that don't have enough basis in fact."

"But we don't know it's not true."

"Here's what we know: Jill wouldn't be a high-value target. There's nobody in her life that could pay some kind of ransom. There's not another good reason someone would go to the trouble to spin up this kind of an offer for her, just in the name of causing trouble. Probably this is the absolute truth."

"But what if—"

"We'll go to Atlanta and follow the trail. That's the next step. Don't think past that right now."

She blew out a breath and dropped her head to his chest, lulled by the slow, steady beat of his heart and the fingers he cupped around her nape. All her runaway thoughts about human trafficking and identity theft were fueled by reading too many fictional thrillers. He wasn't alarmed, so she shouldn't be either.

On a sigh, she straightened and caught a flash of pain on Cressida's face before she could hide it.

Infusing genuine warmth into her tone, Sam

stepped away. "Thank you for your help. I really appreciate it."

Cressida jerked her shoulders. "I don't see that I gave you more than you had already."

"It's something." She didn't quite know what, yet, but it was a direction. "We'll get out of your way now."

After a moment's hesitation, Cressida showed them to the door. As they reached the end of the walk, she called out, "For what it's worth, I hope you find her."

Sam lifted her hand in a wave. "So do I."

* * *

"WHAT WAS THAT?" Griff jerked his head back toward the rapidly disappearing house.

"What was what?"

"At the end. You sounded almost... I don't know. Warm. I know you. That wasn't a fake, you-get-more-flies-with-honey-so-you're-gonna-grit-your-teeth-and-play-nice-with-your-nemesis tone. What changed back there?"

Sam shrugged. "Honestly, I feel sorry for her."

Had she somehow sustained a head injury when he wasn't looking? "You feel *sorry* for her? The woman who made it her mission in life to make yours a living hell all through high school, who spent the weekend taking potshots at you? Why on earth would you feel sorry for her?"

She rolled her head toward him on the seat. "Because she doesn't have you. She might have ended up with money and presumably the status that goes with it, but she doesn't have a husband who looks at her the way you look at me. She's in marriage counseling and on a hefty dose of anti-anxiety and blood pressure meds. I'm not saying her choice to take her misery out on others is acceptable, but I feel sorry for her. She's spent her life chasing the wrong thing, and the price she's paying to keep it is steep."

Griff absorbed that as he navigated back to the highway. One of the things that had always drawn him to Sam was her sweetness. Her willingness to see the best in people. She had such a big heart. At length, he reached out to curl his fingers through hers, bringing her slim hand to his lips. "Your capacity for forgiveness astounds me."

She snorted. "Oh, don't mistake me. I haven't forgiven her for the things she's done to me. She's still a heinous hellbeast. But it seems like karma is properly in action, so I'm letting the rest of it go."

"And that's enough for you?"

"It seems to me it matters more where you end up than where you started. I'm the one back in your bed. That's a silent revenge that's more than enough for me."

He smirked. "Not so silent."

Her unapologetic laugh eased the last of the strain from her face. "Yeah, well, whose fault is that?"

"Am I supposed to apologize for taking great satisfaction in making you scream?"

"God, I hope not. I'd love it if you'd repeat the performance at the earliest opportunity."

Hell yes.

He made an exaggerated survey of their surroundings. "There are no convenient pull-offs, so we should find the nearest hotel."

Her giggle echoed in the car. "Be serious."

"You think I'm kidding?" He could too easily imagine finding a private spot and dragging her out of that seat so she could straddle him in his. The idea of it had his zipper straining.

"We need to strategize what's next. You've been a great sport about all this so far, but even I concede this reactive approach I've had isn't effective. Atlanta may be next, but we need to figure out what we're going to *do* there. It's too huge a place to go at it all scattershot."

Sobering, he switched gears to the practical. "It's too late to head for Atlanta from here. It would be after ten by the time we arrived. Let's find somewhere to stay for the night a bit further down the road, and we'll do that strategizing." And if he made her scream after the strategizing, that seemed like a win-win for them both.

About fifteen miles out of town, he spotted a

sign for Wishful. The name niggled something in the back of his brain, and he'd taken the turn before he remembered why.

"Where are we going?"

"Do you remember that trio of old women we met in Vegas?"

"They'd be hard to forget."

"They were from Wishful. On the flight over, they told me the town has this fountain that allegedly grants wishes."

Even in the fading light, he caught the raised brow. "You never struck me as the kind of guy who believed in such things."

"I don't know if I do, but under the circumstances, I figure we can use all the help we can get with this search, so it can't hurt. And maybe they'll have a hotel. At the very least, they'll have somewhere we can stop for dinner. I'm getting hungry."

"That's as good a reason as any."

Half an hour later, Griff rolled into downtown Wishful. Banners hung from every light pole declaring it *Where hope springs eternal.* A park full of old-growth trees lay at the center of what he presumed was the town square. Pedestrians strolled along sidewalks in front of brightly lit shops and restaurants with autumnal displays in their front windows.

Sam peered out the side window. "Did we just drive onto the set of a Hallmark movie?"

"They've got the charm factor dialed up to eleven, that's for sure. You want to do fountain first or food?"

Her stomach chose that moment to growl. "The creature has spoken, apparently."

"Looks like they've got a diner up there on that corner."

"I could go for a big, fat cheeseburger."

Griff found a parking space. He took her hand as they crossed the park toward the cheery lights of Dinner Belles. Her fingers laced with his, and that palm-to-palm connection felt exactly, perfectly right. Because she was exactly, perfectly right for him, and he wasn't letting go again.

A bell jangled as he dragged open the door.

The place was packed, which meant the food was likely top notch. An older black woman called out from across the room, "Wait's about twenty minutes just now."

Griff nodded. "You want to try to find somewhere else?"

Before Sam could answer, another voice rang out, "Griff! Yoo-hoo, Griff!"

From a corner booth in the back, a familiar group of ladies waved. They all had more silver and white in their hair than they had eight years ago, but he'd have known them anywhere. Grinning, Griff raised his arm in return.

One of the women—his seatmate on the flight to Vegas—slid out of the booth and shuffled over. "Oh, I can't believe it's you! You and your wife simply must join us. How are you, Samantha, dear?"

Sam opened her mouth, apparently at a loss for words. Eyes alight with humor, she smiled up at him. "I'm well. Thank you."

The woman—Miss Betty, Griff remembered —tugged at his arm. "Come, come."

"Oh, no ma'am. We couldn't possibly intrude on your dinner."

"Nonsense. This is kismet. We've got room, and we'd love to catch up."

Griff glanced at Sam, who shrugged. "We'd love to."

As they trailed Miss Betty back to the table, Sam murmured sotto voce, "I can't believe they remember us!"

"Apparently we made an impression."

Miss Betty made fresh introductions. "You remember Delia and Maudie Bell."

"Of course. Great to see you again, ladies." Griff slid in next to Sam.

Miss Maudie Bell, a heavy-boned woman with a booming laugh, banged a hand on the table. "What brings you two to our neck of the woods?"

Before he could decide what version of the truth to share, Sam stepped in. "We're on a bit of a road trip. After we left Oxford this afternoon, we saw the sign and Griff remembered y'all mentioning Wishful, so we thought we'd stop in and check it out."

"We're so glad you did!" Miss Betty exclaimed.

The woman who seemed to be running things stopped at the edge of the table. "Lawd, we're jumpin' tonight. What can I get y'all to drink?"

"Mama Pearl, look here! This is Griff and Samantha—I'm sorry, dear, I've forgotten your last name," Miss Betty said.

"Powell."

"Griff and Samantha Powell."

Damn, that sounded good.

"We met them in Vegas several years ago, just before their wedding," Miss Delia explained.

"Well, we met Griff on the plane. We ran into them before their wedding," Miss Maudie Bell corrected.

Actually, they'd assumed the bit about the wedding. He and Sam hadn't decided to get married until far later that night.

"I've still got those photos we took of you!"

Miss Betty began digging in her voluminous purse. She produced her phone and began swiping. After a moment, she held it up, triumphant. "See?"

Dutifully, Mama Pearl studied the picture. "Y'all made a good lookin' couple. Still do. Drinks?"

"Uh, sweet tea, please," Sam said.

"Same for me. Can I see that, Miss Betty?"

She handed over the phone. He and Sam leaned their heads together. The image on the screen showed them dressed in the finery they'd donned for her friend Chloe's wedding. The rented suit fit his military-honed body like a glove, and the champagne bridesmaid's dress was easily enough mistaken for bridal garb. They stood wrapped around each other, beaming for the camera.

"God, we were so young." Sam reached out, swiping through the few other photos. "So happy."

The undertone of regret for those lost years hit him in the gut. He couldn't stop himself from pressing a kiss to her brow—apology as much as comfort.

She handed the phone back. "Would you mind sending those to us?"

"Oh, of course! We should've thought of it back then. What's your number?"

Sam reeled it off and confirmed receipt of the photos.

Mama Pearl returned with their teas.

Once she'd taken their orders, Miss Delia settled back against the seat. "Do y'all have any children?"

It was a perfectly reasonable question to ask the married couple these women thought them to be. In eight years, most folks would have kids. Griff found himself not wanting to admit to the truth because he didn't want to have to explain exactly how badly he'd fucked everything up. How they weren't married. Didn't have kids.

Sam leaned into him. "Not yet."

Not yet.

His blood fired as his mind flashed back to

this morning. He shifted, willing back his body's response. "We've… uh… got a few things to take care of first."

Like getting married again, sooner rather than later. He just had to find a way to convince her.

CHAPTER 11

"*Y*ou covered our asses beautifully back there."

Dinner had been an utterly surreal affair. Understanding Griff's reluctance to get into any of the details of their relationship, Sam had slid right into the role of his wife without blinking. Maybe it should've alarmed her how easy it was to spin the lie, blending fact with fiction and a healthy dose of the dreams she'd long ago relegated to mental mothballs. The dreams she still wanted.

As they strode back across the town green,

headed toward the fountain, she leaned into his side, appreciating the warm circle of his arm around her. "Does that bother you?"

"No. It was like this glimpse into the life we should have had. Would have had, if not for me."

The guilt dripping in his tone pinched at her heart. There'd been many times over the past eight years she'd thought exactly that. That he'd robbed them of something wonderful. And maybe, if he'd stayed, they'd have gotten some variation of that dream. But she didn't want to dwell in the past, on maybes and what might have beens. Somewhere in the last few days, she'd let go of the hurt and forgiven him. Her soul felt lighter for it, and she wanted that for him. Wanted to ease the burden he'd carried.

She tugged him to a halt, reaching up to frame his face. "Stop. What happened happened. We can't change back then. We can only focus on the now. You're here, Griffin, exactly where you promised you'd be. No matter what happened in between, that's what matters."

His eyes searched her face, and she sensed some inner struggle going on inside him. Questioning whether to believe her? Assessing whether he'd done enough penance to atone for hurting her? What could she do or say to convince him? She'd once thought that simply loving him would be enough. That wasn't nothing. But the complicated reality was that love had to be accepted, and she had no idea if he fully believed he'd earned it. So she resisted the urge to find the right words and willed him to feel the truth of it in her touch.

At length, he dropped his brow to hers, pulling her close. "I love you."

He'd said the words this morning. But she'd said them first, and it was entirely different hearing them while not in a deeply intimate position. She closed her eyes, letting the sweetness of it wash over her. Simple words that weren't at all simple for him to say. He hadn't come from a close-knit family that easily and regularly expressed their affection. His few years with Joan Reynolds hadn't erased all the time and training that emotion was a weakness, a thing to be exploited. With this declaration, he was handing her his heart and the ability to crush it.

Rising to her toes, Sam threaded her fingers in the fine, soft hair at his nape and brushed her lips to his. "I know." Because in this moment, her acceptance and belief in him would mean more than reciprocity. It meant the forgiveness he so desperately craved.

His mouth curved against hers. "How about we do this wish thing and go get a room at The Babylon so I can show you."

She shivered, imagining all the delicious ways he could do exactly that with privacy and time. "I one thousand percent support this plan."

The burble of the fountain was a soothing noise, punctuated by the occasional sound of traffic and pedestrians around the green. Judging by the number of coins that glimmered like a treasure grotto beneath the water, plenty of people bought into the town legend. Maybe that would be good luck. They could use some of that.

Sam dug out some loose change from her purse and handed a coin over to Griff. He curled his big palm around it and stared at the fountain, deep in thought. She found herself studying him as she clutched her own coin. He'd brought her here to wish for help in finding Jill. But it wasn't her friend she thought of now. It was the second chance the search for her had given them.

I wish for this to be the real and true love I thought we found eight years ago.

Before she could think better of it or let the guilt seep in, she let the coin drop. It hit with a deep, resonant *plunk*. Griff flicked his toward the fall of water at the center, watching it for long moments after it disappeared.

"What did you wish for?"

He glanced over, his face inscrutable. "The ladies were very clear you're not supposed to tell, or it won't come true."

"Fair enough."

His fingers laced with hers again. "C'mon. We have other things to think about tonight."

She thrilled at the promise in his voice and followed him back to the car.

The Babylon Hotel and Spa was lush and gorgeous and wholly unexpected for a town this size. Sam wanted to look everywhere at once, admiring the beautiful finishes and fixtures. And as the doors to the elevator closed behind them, her heart began to pound, remembering another elevator ride in another posh hotel. She thought maybe Griff would back her against the wall of the car and get started on that walk down memory lane, but he stayed where he was, perfectly still. A stranger might've thought he was relaxed, but she could see the leashed tension, like a lion waiting to pounce. She rubbed her thighs together, knowing she was the prey. God, she couldn't wait.

The elevator doors slid open. With every step down the plush, carpeted hall, her heart thudded harder. Griff slid the keycard into the lock, opening the door to a suite with a sprawling king-size bed. Everything about the space shouted luxury and comfort. The heavy door fell shut behind them, latching with the kind of thud that spoke of good soundproofing.

The click of the lock was like a starter pistol. They both dropped their bags and dove for each other, mouths crashing and fusing as greedy hands touched and took. Clothes were shed in a fevered dance until they were both naked and gasping. Yes, *this* was the kind of desperation she'd always wanted from him.

He lifted her up, and she wrapped her legs around his hips as he pressed her back against the wall. It was unexpected and absolutely thrilling.

"Okay?" he rasped.

"God, yes." She could feel his crown notched at her entrance and wanted all of him. "Take me."

On a growl that was almost feral, he thrust into her. Her head fell back on a gasp at the delicious, blunt intrusion. His hands under her legs clenched.

"Samantha?" Even now, when his desire was barely leashed, he had enough control to take care of her.

"I'm okay. I'm okay. Just don't stop."

And he didn't. He set a frenzied pace, plunging into her over and over, taking them on a fast, reckless rise that left her in no doubt that she was being claimed. She gloried in it, riding the flood of pleasure until she crested and cried out his name, her body clamping down and demanding release from his.

Sam came back to herself slowly, feeling his sweat-slicked skin pressed to hers, his muscled chest heaving.

"Okay?" he croaked.

Limply, she tried to stroke a hand across his shoulder. "I... think I might have died. I'm pretty okay with it, though."

The rumble of his laugh shook them both, setting off aftershocks that had her eyes crossing.

"I meant to take more time with you."

She managed to lift her head. "I mean… we do have all night." She hoped they had forever, but she wouldn't push for that. Not yet.

Humor and renewed heat lit his gaze as he spun away from the wall. "Thank God."

And he tumbled them onto the bed.

MORNING CAME FAR TOO SOON. Griff woke with it, as usual, but he didn't budge. Not with Sam tucked up close, skin to skin, her face only inches from his on the pillow. He'd never take this for granted. Waking up with her. Seeing the long fan of her lashes cast shadows against her cheeks. Feeling her feet wedged beneath his legs, her hand over his heart. Everyday intimacies he hadn't known he'd crave.

He craved everything about this woman.

A weak stripe of sunlight fell from a gap in the curtains and slowly crawled up from the foot of the bed. It had reached her shoulders by the time her eyes fluttered open. He watched as the blur of sleep shifted to awareness and relief. It was the relief that did him in. Because a part of her still expected him to be gone when she woke. He'd done that to her. And he'd spend the rest of his life making it up to her, if she'd let him.

"Morning, Sleeping Beauty."

She closed the scant distance between them, snuggling close. "Does it have to be?"

Combing his fingers through her silky hair, Griff pressed a kiss to her temple. "I'd love nothing more than to stay here with you for the next year or two, but we've still got to sort out our plan of attack for Atlanta. Sorry for distracting you from that last night."

She pulled back and shot him an arch look. "Which time?"

"I'd say all of them, but I'd be lying."

"Well, I can't exactly complain about the sex coma you left me in, so we'll just both admit we enjoyed ourselves and move on." With a smacking kiss, she rolled away. "I need a vat of coffee and a shower to get my brain working. We'll figure out the plan on the road."

Forty-five minutes later, they were rolling toward Georgia, to-go cups of coffee from Wishful's coffee shop, The Daily Grind, in the center console. Sam opened her laptop and began to make a list.

"So, obviously options include going by her apartment and canvassing her neighborhood to see if any of her neighbors have seen her. But that doesn't necessarily seem like the best use of our time. If she hasn't been home since the festival, then they aren't likely to have any information for us."

Griff tapped at the steering wheel, considering. "Then let's review what we know and see if we can't narrow things down. Jill was planning on coming to the bachelorette weekend until she received an opportunity to sub for some band we don't know the name of, for the festival in Gatlinburg over the weekend. As it seems like she didn't go home to Atlanta, we conclude the band was happy with her performance, and she joined them on the next leg of their tour, which could be literally anywhere. Has she posted any status updates since yesterday?"

Her fingers flew over the keys for a few minutes. "No. And I'm not finding her tagged by anyone else recently, so there are no clues there."

"Assuming she did get the tour gig, she'd be gone for a while, I'd think. Who would she have to notify?"

"Logically, her boss and the band she's been playing with the past couple of years."

"Do we know who they are?"

Sam winced. "I should know that as her friend, but I don't. She's been working as a barista at a Starbucks somewhere. No idea which one. There have to be dozens of them in her corner of Atlanta alone."

Again, not an efficient use of their limited time. Griff didn't know how long Sam could devote to this search, but he knew their window was closing. "She might have just taken leave or even quit without telling them why."

"Hmm. Maybe I can track down the band. Surely, she'd have posted something about them or with them on social media at some point." She went silent, her eyes narrowing on the screen the way he remembered when she was deep in research mode.

"Ah ha! The band is called Crystal Sundown."

"What kind of music is that, anyway?"

"Looks like some kind of bluesy indie rock. And the lead guitarist works at a bookstore in Marietta."

He gave her the side eye. "Your Google stalking skills are impressive."

"I'm good at finding information. And most people have way more out there than they realize." She whipped out her phone and dialed. The call rang over the car's Bluetooth.

"Thank you for calling Peachtree Books. This is Rhonda speaking. How may I help you?"

"Yes, I was trying to reach Clive Taylor."

"He's not here right now."

"Do you know if he'll be in later today?"

"His shift starts at noon."

"Great. Thank you." She hung up, looking triumphant. "That gives us just enough time to get there."

They strode through the doors of Peachtree Books at a quarter to one. It was a trendy, independent bookstore with a vaguely industrial vibe. A small coffee shop took up one corner of the main floor. A second half floor stretched above them, reached by a spiral metal staircase to one side. It was the kind of place he knew Sam would normally linger and browse. But today, she was a woman on a mission.

She made a beeline for a slim guy with slicked-back hair and a hipster beard who wore the pale orange apron that designated him as a store employee. "Excuse me, I'm looking for Clive."

"I'm Clive. Can I help you?"

Since his gaze slipped over to Griff, he

picked up the questioning. "You're lead guitarist for Crystal Sundown?"

Clive brightened. "Yes. Are you looking to book a gig?"

"No actually. We're looking for Jill Dunham."

His face clouded. "Well, you won't find that turncoat here. She up and left us high and dry."

"She quit the band?" Sam asked.

"Yeah. Left us for a better option." Bitterness dripped from his tone like venom.

Hopefully that would make him more likely to talk. Griff crossed his arms. "Do you know who?"

"Why?"

"We're friends of hers," Sam explained. "We haven't been able to reach her in days, and we're worried."

Clive snorted. "She probably dropped you, too. She'd do damn near anything to play with Smokin' Orleans."

"You're sure that's who she's touring with?" Griff prompted.

"That's what she said. Can't really blame her, I guess." The concession was reluctant.

"Thank you, Clive. You've been a big help."

"Yeah. Thanks, man."

"Sure. Whatever."

Sam had her phone out before they even got back to the door. "According to their tour schedule, Smokin' Orleans went from Gatlinburg to Memphis and on to..." she trailed off, her brows drawing together.

"What?"

She met his gaze, her own filled with amusement and something he couldn't quite read. "They're playing Las Vegas tonight."

Vegas. Everything, it seemed, pointed back to Vegas. And maybe that was fitting. Back to the beginning. Back where he'd screwed up. So he could get it right this time.

"Well... we might as well follow this through."

"I'll book the flight."

CHAPTER 12

They made a mid-afternoon flight. Barely. The mad dash through the concourse left Sam swearing she'd get back to the gym for something other than yoga. She was still winded as she crossed the jet bridge. Griff hadn't even broken a sweat. Of course.

From the moment they'd gotten a location, everything had been go-go-go action. There'd been no time to think. She hadn't really allowed herself to think since the whole search started. But as she settled into the window seat and buckled her safety belt, the whole thing started catching up to her.

She was on a plane to Vegas—somewhere she'd sworn she'd never go again—with the very man who was the reason for that edict.

Because something like panic was licking at her heels, she'd made excuses, pulling out her laptop to catch up on grading for the job she also wasn't thinking about this week. She'd always been good at losing herself in work, shutting everything else out. When she surfaced again a few hours later, Griff was dozing, his hands folded over those washboard abs.

She studied him, drinking in the strong line of his jaw, the faint peek of ink at the collar of his shirt from the tattoos she'd traced with her fingers. And her tongue. He was every inch a warrior in repose. God, he was beautiful. She'd always thought so. There was a gravity to him now that he hadn't had when they were together before. No doubt from whatever he'd seen and done as part of his service. She hadn't asked him about it, and he hadn't volunteered.

But she'd felt the scars hidden beneath the ink and wondered how else the experience had marked him.

He wasn't the same insecure boy he'd been in high school. Wasn't the same young Marine looking for purpose he'd been at twenty-two. From the moment he'd walked back into her life, every action, every word, had demonstrated constancy and a commitment to truly giving them another shot. But she couldn't stop the curl of anxiety deep in her gut. Vegas was where everything had changed between them before. Would things change there again? Would it be the end of this wild ride? Would she wake up and find this was all a dream?

"You're thinking awfully hard there, Professor." Griff opened his eyes, focused on her. His lazy smile faded, and he reached for her hand. "Hey. You okay?"

Sam focused on the warmth of his grip, closing her eyes for a moment.

"Samantha?"

"Sorry. I'm just..." How could she share these

fears with him without exacerbating his guilt and potentially triggering his issues with self-worth? "We're going to Vegas."

His lips twitched. "Yeah. If you're having second thoughts, you missed the window to speak a few hours ago. I don't think you want to pull a D.B. Cooper."

She wasn't in the mood for hijacker humor. "No. It's not that. It just feels weird."

It wasn't the same as before. Sure, her trip back then had also started with bridesmaid duties, and then happenstance had thrown them into a fake relationship that they'd wanted to make real. That unexpected weekend had led to some of the best memories of her life. And one of the worst.

"Fair enough," he conceded. "Have you ever been back?"

She shook her head. "I could never go there with anyone but you. Everything about it is a reminder of our time together. I spent so long trying not to think about it, and now I'm going with you, and it's just... bringing up a lot of...

stuff."

Way to be articulate, Dr. Ferguson.

He stroked his thumb along the back of her hand. "I wish I could go back and change how I handled things."

The temptation to fall down the rabbit hole of what if scenarios was enormous. But the pursuit of it would only hurt them both.

"I mean… of course a part of me does, too. But I'm not bringing this up to talk about re-grets. I'm just remembering. I haven't let myself do that in years. Not really. But being here right now with you, I remember how it felt to be her." She hit a key on her laptop and pointed to the wedding day photo she'd made her desktop wallpaper.

"I loved you so much I was blinded by it. And I think that's exactly what you were afraid of. But we're not kids anymore, Griffin. I see you clearer than I could at twenty-two, and I still love you. Mistakes, flaws, and all. I need you to know that. To believe it. Because I don't really know how it will feel to walk those streets again, by your side, and I don't want you to think I regret being with you again. Because I don't. I'm glad we have interfering friends who didn't tell us we'd be seeing each other, because I would have come up with an excuse, and I would have missed out on all of this. I can't think of a bigger regret than that."

Tension drained out of him as he pressed his brow to hers. "Samantha, I—"

"Attention passengers. Please return your carryons to the overhead bins or under the seat in front of you and fasten your seatbelts. We're about to begin our descent to Las Vegas."

"Nearly there," Griff murmured.

She waited for him to continue, wondering what he'd been about to say. But he didn't, so she stowed her laptop and settled in for the remainder of the flight, fingers laced with his.

Once they'd landed, they took the tram from Concourse D to the main part of the airport. They hadn't checked any bags, but Sam found herself slowing as they reached baggage claim.

"Right over there. That was where I saw you again." He'd hauled her ridiculously over-sized bag off the baggage carousel.

"I thought you didn't recognize me."

"Ha! Seeing you was an absolute sucker punch. You always made me so nervous, and suddenly there you were, bigger than life and so very..."

"Cocky?" he suggested.

"Potent. I thought I'd trip all over my tongue trying to talk to you. It was like being in high school all over again."

Griff smirked, looking, for a moment, like the teenage boy he'd been. "You always did have the prettiest blush."

She stared. "You made me blush on purpose?"

"As often as possible. It was one of my favorite teenage hobbies."

"Sadist." She went to goose him in the ribs, but he only twisted away, laughing before hauling her into his side and pressing a smacking kiss to her cheek.

The playfulness eased a knot in her chest, and she cuddled closer, her arm around his waist, her finger hooking on one of his belt loops. "It just occurred to me. You weren't on my flight in, and I don't think you'd actually checked your bag. Why were you even over there?"

"I spotted you on my way out the door, and I had to see if it was really you."

So it hadn't been a hundred percent chance. He'd sought her out instead of going the other way. "Thank God for healthy curiosity. You saved me from a hella uncomfortable weekend as the only single at Chloe's wedding." She didn't want to think about the potential misery of that scenario.

"You saved me from a probably ill-advised decision to come out here on my own."

They started toward the car rental counters. "Why *did* you decide to come to Vegas when you got out? Given how much you despise gambling because of your dad, it seems a really odd place to choose."

"Well, I wasn't kidding about the all-you-can-eat buffets. But beyond that, I guess I wanted to test myself. Make sure I didn't have any of him in me."

Always trying to prove himself. Sam squeezed his hand. "You're nothing like your father."

"That's good to hear, since I've tried damned hard not to be. C'mon. Let's get a car and get on into town. We've only got a few hours before the show to track down Jill."

Reminded of their purpose, Sam shoved her anxieties back into a box. She was being ridiculous. There was nothing to worry about here. At least, not with Griff. Maybe they were still sorting things out between them, but they were solid now in a way they hadn't been eight years ago. If they were going to make it, she had to trust him again. Might as well start now.

"THAT'S the last of the major hotels and resorts in town." Sam dropped her phone onto the bed. "None of them has a reservation for Jill Dunham, and no one would admit to housing Smokin' Orleans."

"Not a surprise. If she just joined the tour, reservations wouldn't likely be under her name, and the band probably registered with fake names, anyway. Assuming they're in a hotel and didn't rent a house somewhere."

"Was that something Kyle did on tour?"

"Sure. He was on a kick of using famous cowboys from the Old West by the time I came on board. Apparently, he'd run out of aliases that the Winchester brothers used on *Supernatural*."

She snorted a laugh. "Well, you said finding out where she was staying would be a long shot. Did you have any luck finding tickets to the show?"

"Show's sold out. Which doesn't matter. We wouldn't be able to get near her that way without VIP passes, and I don't think we want to drop a grand or more for those."

Her mouth fell open. "Seriously?"

"It's big money. Of course, that's for the headlining band. They don't sell separate ones for the opening acts."

"So now what? Do we see if we can find ticket scalpers?"

"No guarantee we'd get seats close enough to the stage to see she's there. And aside from that, we didn't come all this way to not actually talk to her."

"Where does that leave us?"

He'd been giving that some consideration. "We know the venue, and I know how things work behind the curtain. I'm gonna try to get us in the back."

"What? We're just gonna try to sneak in? This seems rather more complicated than getting into the athletic locker to replace all the air in the balls with helium."

Griff's lips twitched. "I feel like my capacity for covert operations is being impugned. But that aside, no, we're not going to sneak. Sneaking looks suspicious. We're going to walk in as if we belong there. A big part of infiltration is confidence."

Sam looked askance in his direction. "Really?"

He gestured to his habitual dark jeans and long-sleeved black T-shirt. "This was basically my uniform when I was on tour with Kyle as his bodyguard."

"What about me? Nobody's going to think I'm security." She was still wearing the jeans and sweater she'd put on that morning.

"Nope. You're gonna need a wardrobe change."

Because it was Vegas, they found a boutique in the hotel lobby.

"What are we looking for?" she asked.

Griff riffled through the racks. "Something for a night out. You'll be acting in the capacity of a special guest of Smokin' Orleans." Finding what he wanted, he shoved it toward her.

She arched a brow but said nothing, only

checking the size and swapping it out before disappearing into the dressing room. Flagging down a salesclerk, he pointed to the dress. "She's going to need shoes and one of those little useless purses that just hold an ID and a lipstick or whatever."

"A clutch. Size on the shoes?"

"Seven and a half," Sam called.

"On it." The clerk disappeared.

"I don't know about this," Sam muttered.

"Just wait until you have the whole thing," Griff urged.

A minute later, the woman came back and slid a shoebox past the curtain. There was a rustle and some muttering. Then Sam jerked the curtain open and stepped out, doing a little twirl.

Griff nearly swallowed his tongue.

The dress was silver, conservatively cut girl-next-door from the front, but the back. Dear God in heaven. The back dipped low, almost to her waist, leaving a tantalizing swath of skin bare, including a clear view of her tattoo. And the shoes… Every single thought left his mind, save how he could get her out of this dress.

"Well? Do I pass muster?"

"You—" When his voice croaked, he had to stop and clear his throat. "You look fucking amazing."

"Now just add this." The clerk came back, handing over a tiny purse. She nodded in satisfaction. "Yes. Excellent choice, sir." Her gaze swung to him, assessing. "You're going to need a jacket."

"Oh, no I—"

"You cannot go out with her looking like *that* without stepping up your own look. With those shoulders, you look like a 48 long." She strode over to a rack, slipping a black coat off a hanger. "Here."

Feeling a little helpless, he looked to Sam.

She shrugged. "When in Vegas."

"Fair enough." He put the jacket on.

The clerk nodded again. "Perfect fit."

"Mmm." Sam's hum of confirmation sounded more like a purr, and the look she gave him said her mind was just as distracted from their mission as his.

"We'll take all of it," Griff said.

Fifteen minutes later, they'd stowed Sam's street clothes in their room and headed out the door. The moment they hit the sidewalk, the energy of the Strip pulsed around him. Along with it came a healthy burst of nostalgia. He'd cared for Sam long before running into each other in that airport, but this was where he'd slid the rest of the way in love with her. This was where he'd dared to dream they could make something together. And he hoped it would be where they solidified the renewal of their commitment to each other. But he couldn't turn his mind to that plan until they'd done what they came here to do.

The venue wasn't far. As it was still a bit more than an hour before the show, the crowds weren't bad and full security wasn't yet in place. They skirted around to the back of the building. He kept Sam close, as much because he wanted his hand on her as to avoid the security cameras he spotted. Buses and trucks with trailers filled the smaller parking lot. Equipment would have been offloaded well before now, so there'd be no blending in with the staff that way. Still, it couldn't hurt to check the back doors, in case some careless person had left one unlocked, or propped open.

Griff sent up a prayer of thanks as one nearby opened and someone stepped out for a smoke break. Lengthening his stride, he caught the door before it could close, nodding a greeting to the skinny dude he pegged as a tech. With one hand, he gestured Sam inside, appreciating the rear view again as she moved past him into the fluorescent lit interior.

"Hey! You can't be in here."

Of course, their luck would run out here. This was why he didn't gamble.

"Let me do the talking," he murmured, neatly sliding in front of Sam as he turned to face the muscle-bound guy stalking toward them.

A quick visual assessment of his movements

told Griff he could handle himself. Former cop or military. No uniform, so he was unlikely venue security. Bodyguard with the talent? With Smokin' Orleans or the headlining band? If Griff guessed wrong, they'd be unceremoniously booted out on their asses.

He lifted his hands in a non-threatening manner. "Not here to cause trouble, man. I just have a guest to bring back for Miss Dunham with Smokin' Orleans. She told us to come in the back."

"There's no Miss Dunham with Smokin' Orleans. Get out."

Well shit.

Sam stepped out from behind him. "Wait, wait. Jill Dunham. This woman." She flashed her phone toward him. "She may be using a stage name."

The bodyguard's gaze slid over Sam, eyes flaring with interest, and suddenly Griff wished he hadn't insisted on the change of clothes. He fought not to curl his hands into fists. The man finally shifted his attention to the phone. A faint lightening of his expression said he recognized Jill.

"That picture could have come from anywhere."

"Please, can you just let her know we're here?" Sam asked. "We're not trying to see anyone else."

He looked her over again. "You can go back. He has to leave."

"Not a chance in hell." Griff stepped in front of her.

Sam gripped his arm, trying to tug him around. "But I just need to see her for a little while. You could wait—"

"No." This wasn't something he'd negotiate about.

Temper lit her eyes, but he turned away, back to the bodyguard.

"Will you take a note to her?"

The guy's expression turned smug. "Man, I don't have time to play delivery boy. This is the option. Take it or leave it."

"We're leaving." Griff grabbed Sam's hand.

"But—"

"We're. Leaving."

He towed her back out the door and into the parking lot. She waited only until they'd cleared the first row of vehicles before blowing up.

"What the hell? That was our opening. I could be finding her right now."

Griff rounded on her. "Or you could be walking straight into a sexual assault."

Sam's head kicked back, her eyes going wide.

"Did you not see how that asswipe was looking at you? You don't send single women backstage on their own. Not every band or every venue is like that, but plenty are, and I don't know these people. I'm not sending you into a situation where you could get hurt." Not ever again. She was too fucking precious to risk that way.

Her cheeks paled. "But Jill is back there. We got that much out of him. What if she's not safe?"

Struggling to rein himself in, Griff softened

his tone. "She's safer as part of the talent than an unattached woman would be. She'll be with the rest of the band. With hair and makeup. Costuming. We'll find another way. She'll be tied up with back room meet and greet stuff after the show, so she won't have time to see anyone until after the VIPs are handled. At worse we tail her after that to figure out where she's going. The next tour date isn't until Friday, so they probably won't be leaving out tonight. There's time. I promise we'll find her. But do not ask me to let you walk into danger."

She stared at him for a long moment. "Okay." Shoulders slumping, she heaved a sigh. "So what now?"

"Now we go back for the car."

CHAPTER 13

"*I* am not made for stakeouts." Sam shifted in the front seat of their rental car, wishing she were in yoga pants instead of this dress. Wishing, too, that she hadn't gone for that extra bottle of water. It wasn't like there was a bathroom anywhere nearby. "How can you just sit there?"

Griff didn't take his eyes off the exit where the bands would leave from, but she caught the flicker of a smile. "Practice. A couple hours in a cushy car after a solid dinner is nothing to days in the desert."

"Didn't you get bored? Have trouble paying attention? You could barely sit through classes back in high school."

"Yeah. But that was the job. And I'd still take the quiet of the desert over Mrs. Newberry's droning, any day."

Their junior year English teacher had given Ben Stein a run for his money. Even so, Sam couldn't imagine it. "I think I'd have tried to sneak in a book or... something."

"Can't watch what you're supposed to watch if you're reading."

"How did you pass the time?"

"If it wasn't a posting where we had to be quiet, we talked. Otherwise, I mentally recited a lot of poetry."

Sam shot him the side eye. "Be serious."

He went brows up. "I am. How do you think I could whip out Shelley at dinner that time?"

His public flirting with poetry at Chloe's rehearsal dinner had nearly made her spontaneously combust. "I was too busy having my nerd fantasies come true to question at the time."

That coaxed out a full-on grin. "I knew you'd love that."

"I thought you were laying it on as proof of our fake relationship."

"Sure, I was. But it was the hardest damned thing not to kiss you right then and there."

"Probably a good thing you didn't. I was thinking really hard about jumping you, and that would've been super awkward with an audience."

His rich, rolling laugh filled the car. "Damn, that would've been something. You'd never really flirted with me before that dinner, and I remember thinking I was in so much trouble."

"Why trouble?"

The gaze he turned in her direction was full of heat. "Because I was still trying to keep my hands off you."

Just that one look was enough to have desire curling low in her belly. Sam crossed her legs. "Well, thank God I managed to override your misplaced convictions. I wanted your hands on me."

"A fact I am grateful for everyday."

He wanted her. That had seemed like a miracle at twenty-two, after years of what she'd thought was an unrequited crush. The years since then only seemed to have honed that yearning to a knife's edge. But there was so much more between them than heat, and it was that fueling the questions still circling her brain.

"Can I ask you something?"

"Sure."

She hoped she wasn't about to step in it, but she needed to know. "You got out months ago. Why didn't you come to find me sooner?"

The humor faded from his face, and he turned back to watch the exit. She was on the verge of retracting the question when he finally answered.

"I wanted to have my life together before I came to you. Or how was I any different than I was eight years ago? I knew you were a professor—"

"You looked me up?"

"No. I just know you finish what you start. I never gave into the temptation to look you up all these years. I was too afraid of what I might find. A husband. Kids. The life I gave up." He shook his head. "I wasn't in a place I could handle that when I got out."

She'd wanted all of that. Had sought it out since he'd left her. But no one had ever tempted her to cross that line and make a commitment. No one but him.

"You know, for a guy who hates gambling, you made a hell of a wager that I wouldn't have any of those things after all this time."

"I know. Hence needing to work on my shit. Kyle gave me a chance to do that."

"Was there a lot of shit to work on from your service?" In these past days with him, she hadn't seen any signs of the issues her brother struggled with.

"No. I'm mostly proud of the work I did the second go-round. The adjustment was almost all about rejoining the civilian world. I was luckier than many to have all my brothers to fall back on."

"I'm sure it helped that the separation was your choice. Jonah's having a hard time with that aspect."

"He was injured?"

"Yeah. We don't know all the details, of course. Classified missions and all that, so not where or how or even what exactly happened. He had a severe head injury and complications from shrapnel. At the end of the day, the Navy didn't declare him fit to return to duty."

"That's tough."

"Yeah. And it's hard on Mom, and me too, because we're thrilled he'll finally be out of the line of fire. I think he resents that because it's like we're celebrating the end of his dream. And I get that. But I'm sure as hell not going to apologize for being relieved that he's no longer in a position where he might die from his job every day." Just thinking about it had her shoulders bunching.

Griff took her hand, curling his fingers around hers. "You said he's in Syracuse?"

Soothed by the touch, Sam released a breath. "Yeah, Audrey—she's one of my best friends—created an experimental treatment program for military veterans struggling with PTSD, depression, and anxiety. He's part of the first cohort." She crossed her legs again, trying to get comfortable.

Griff squeezed her hand. "I'm sure he'll come through fine. He's a strong guy."

"No, it's not that. I can't just sit here and wait anymore. I have to find a bathroom."

"Oh. Well, the concert should be wrapping soon."

"Then hopefully the venue will let me in to use their facilities." She let him go and popped her seatbelt. "I'll be fast. Promise."

"I'm coming with you."

Knowing better than to try to talk him out

of his bodyguard mentality, she shoved out of the car and made a beeline for the front doors.

A bored-looking woman sat just inside. "Tickets please?"

"We don't have any," Sam admitted. "I was really just hoping to use the restroom."

"No tickets, no admittance."

"Please?" She clasped her hands in supplication. "I swear I'm not here to see whatever show is here. I really just need the bathroom." She added a restless bounce that was a universal sign of a full bladder.

The woman glanced at Griff.

"He can stay here. Proof I'll be back in just a couple minutes." Sam shot him a significant look. If he tried to say going to the bathroom wasn't safe, they were going to have words.

The woman checked her watch. "Show's nearly over, anyway. Go ahead. Down the hall to the right."

"Thank you! Be right back." She hoofed it as fast as she could manage in the sky-high heels.

Only a few stalls were occupied. She bolted into one and shut the door.

"—you going to Tito's after the concert? Smokin' Orleans is playing a bonus set there tonight."

Sam perked up, tuning into the conversation happening by the sinks at the other end.

"Really?"

"Yeah, they just announced it on their Twitter stream. Small and intimate. The way they're meant to be enjoyed."

Sam's pulse picked up, and she strained to hear more. The sound of running water drowned out the rest of the conversation, and by the time she'd finished her business, the women had left the restroom.

Quickly washing her hands, she whipped out her phone to check Smokin' Orleans' Twitter feed. Sure enough, they'd invited fans out for a bonus show at some place called Tito's Cantina as soon as the bigger show was wrapped. A quick Google search showed it was located close to downtown Las Vegas.

This was the break they needed.

She hurried back to Griff. "I know where they're going to be!"

"Tito's."

Her mouth fell open. "How did you know?"

He jerked his thumb at the woman who'd let them in. "Carlyn here gave me the skinny since we missed the show. I figure we've got just enough time to get down there and grab a table, so we're front and center when the band shows up."

"Then what are we waiting for?"

Tito's was crowded enough that they didn't quite make the front when Smokin' Orleans took the tiny stage, but Sam was close enough to lay eyes on her missing friend as she filed in with the other musicians. Relief and excitement spilled through her, and she shot out of her seat. "Jill!"

On stage, Jill's step faltered. She spun toward the audience, scanning the crowd. Sam waved wildly, suddenly glad of the bright silver of her dress. Jill's eyes widened, her mouth

falling open. After a brief word with the guitarist, she made a beeline over to them.

"Sam! Oh my God, what are you doing
here?"

Sam hauled her in for a tight hug. "Girl, we
have been over half the country trying to track
you down."

She pulled back. "We?"

"Hey, Jill." Griff rose from his seat, flashing
her a smile.

"Well, holy shit."

He pulled her in for a one-armed hug. "I've
been co-detective on this trip."

Sam bit back a laugh as Jill struggled to si-
multaneously play it cool and shoot I-have-so-
many-questions looks in her direction. That
could certainly wait.

"I've been trying to reach you since Friday.
Phone, email, social media. We didn't know
where you were, and when you didn't show at
the bachelorette weekend, I got worried."

"I emailed Cressida. Did that hellbeast not
actually tell anybody?"

"Not until she found your email in spam on Sunday. Why didn't you call me back? Email? Something? I've been frantic."

"I had to pack in a hurry, and I left my phone charger. Everything happened so fast, I haven't had time to deal with getting a new one. I had no idea you were looking for me." She shot another look at Griff. "Both of you?"

"It's a long story." He nodded toward the stage, where the guitarist was making a hurry-up gesture. "I think you're being summoned."

Jill backpedaled a step. "I gotta go. Are you staying for the show?"

Sam automatically leaned into Griff as he put his arm around her. "After all this, we wouldn't miss it."

With one last look that made it absolutely clear explanations would be demanded later, Jill joined her new bandmates on stage.

"Well, that's mission accomplished," Griff murmured, pressing a kiss to her temple as they took their seats again.

She looked up at him. "You've been an awfully good sport about this whole thing. I know I went kind of overboard on this search."

He skimmed her hair back from her face. "Like I said before, I had nowhere more important to be than with you."

God, that felt so good to hear. And it made it easier to admit what had been circling around in the back of her brain all day. "I think, maybe, I needed an excuse to skip over all the hard, awkward parts of starting over with you. This trip was a way to get out of my own way and spend time with you."

His lips curved into that heart-stopping smile. "I can't argue with the outcome. You have your classes squared away for the rest of the week, right?"

"Yeah."

"Then spend the rest of it here with me. No mission but us."

Heart thumping, she let her own smile bloom. "That sounds like the best mission of all."

* * *

OVER A POST-SHOW BREAKFAST at an all-night diner, Griff and Sam filled Jill in on their adventure.

"I can't believe you went to all that trouble to find me."

Griff didn't miss the little hitch in Jill's voice. And that said so much about how few people were regularly looking out for her. She hadn't had a Joan or a network of found family to fall back on. Everything she'd achieved had been almost entirely on her own. She didn't expect people to care.

"We were worried," he said simply.

"I'm so grateful you were willing to do it, but I hate that you both had to take more time off work and accrue all those travel expenses."

"My peace of mind was definitely worth all of that." Sam grabbed the last slice of bacon from her plate and bit in. "And I'm thrilled that it turned out you disappeared for a good reason. I had all kinds of awful scenarios in my head."

Amusement lit Jill's cat-like green eyes. "Have you been bingeing on thrillers again?"

"You know that's my go-to during the mid-semester slump."

Shoving aside the remains of her pancakes, Jill leaned her elbows on the table. "I'd say you can't claim a mid-semester slump now." She waved a finger between the two of them. "I want to know when this happened." There was curiosity and also a little worry in her eyes.

He and Sam hadn't discussed what they were, or what to tell other people. Labels hadn't been necessary up to now. Jill was their first intersection with normal life. The first person who mattered to find out about their involvement. Griff didn't think it would change anything between them, but he sat back and let Sam field the question, so she could answer with as little or as much detail as she wanted.

She picked up the white ceramic mug and

blew on her freshly refilled coffee, an innocent expression on her face. "Which time?"

Jill's brows practically hit her hairline. "This has happened before? Girl, you've been holding out on me."

Griff couldn't be offended by that. As far as he knew, Sam had never told a soul about their brief marriage. He hadn't told many, and definitely nobody from home until his brothers had guessed.

"This actually isn't our first time in Vegas together."

How far would she go with this story?

Jill frowned, thinking back. "You were in a wedding here after college, weren't you?"

"Mmhmm. Griff was my date."

The frown shifted to incredulity. "How did I not know this?"

"It was kind of last minute," Griff offered.

"Still! You had a thing for him forever. How did you never tell me after?"

Sam shrugged. "Because what happened in Vegas stayed in Vegas." There was no rancor in her tone, just easy acceptance. Maybe she really had moved beyond the pain he'd caused her. That was something worth celebrating.

Jill folded her arms, face pulled into an exaggerated pout. "I feel like this violates the best friend code."

"Don't feel left out. I never told anybody we got married."

"You're *married!*" Her shriek cut off conversation across the restaurant. All the diners at nearby tables stared in their direction, waiting for drama to unfold. Jill had the good grace to hunch her shoulders and blush.

"We were," Griff corrected quietly.

She sat back in her seat, a myriad of expressions flickering over her features. What had happened between "I do" and "I don't"? Who had ended things? Both were fair questions, but not what she finally asked. "So now you're… what?"

At Sam's hesitation, something knotted in his chest. Would she actually balk at defining them? Was she rethinking all the rash decisions that had led to this point?

She leaned into him, a smile curving that pretty mouth. "Starting over."

It was the perfect answer. No more and no less than the truth. The tension in him released. This felt like the passing of some test or hurdle. Griff draped his arm along the back of the booth and pressed a kiss to the top of Sam's head, loving her little hum of pleasure.

Jill watched the display with speculation. "Well, congratulations to you both. I don't have to ask if you're happy. That's obvious."

It meant something that she could see it. But Griff knew this likely wouldn't be the end of it.

Sam's "Thanks" was split by a jaw-cracking. yawn. "Oh my God, I'm so tired. This is so far past my bedtime. Are y'all leaving out for the next leg of the tour tomorrow? Uh... Today?"

"No, we've got a couple days here, so I can finally deal with my phone and pick up some more clothes and stuff."

"Will you have time for lunch or dinner or

something before you leave? I was really looking forward to catching up last weekend."

"I can probably manage something."

He could facilitate that something. "You could go with her for the shopping." That would free him up to set his own plans in motion.

"Are you sure? I promised we'd spend the rest of the week together."

Griff smiled, toying with the ends of her hair. If he got his way, they'd be spending the rest of their lives together. "There's time, Professor. I can entertain myself for a few hours. Y'all go have a catch up."

The server brought the check, and they made plans for where and when to meet.

Sam slid out of the booth. "I'm gonna visit the ladies before we head back to the hotel. Be right back."

Griff and Jill both watched until she disappeared down the corridor. When he turned back, he found her studying him with a cool-eyed stare.

Here it came.

"Go ahead and ask."

"What are your intentions toward my friend?"

He opted for bald honesty. "I'm in love with her. I've been in love with her since we were twenty-two. My intention is to get my wife back and spend the next sixty or so years making up for fucking things up the first time."

Jill blinked at him. "Wow."

Griff's lips twitched. "Does that meet your approval?"

After a long moment, she nodded. "Yeah, I'd say it does."

"Good. Because I could use your help."

"Oh?"

He quickly outlined what he needed. She was grinning by the end. "Oh, I am in."

"In for what?" Sam slid back into her seat.

"Dinner tomorrow night." The lie rolled off his tongue easily. "I promised to introduce her to that Japanese place we ate at all those years ago."

"Oh, yes, please. It was delicious. Meanwhile, I need a bed. I'm about asleep on my feet."

He stood, tugging her up and into him. Her head automatically nestled against his shoulder. God, she was cute when she was tired. "C'mon, Professor. Let's go before you turn into a pumpkin."

"Good idea."

They collectively made their way outside.

"You're sure we can't drop you off?" Griff asked.

"Nah, it's in the opposite direction of your hotel. I'll get an Uber."

Sam drowsed against him, her fingers hooked into his belt loops again as they waited for the driver. Griff loved that easy, unconscious show of possession.

When the car arrived, Sam released him long enough to hug Jill. "I'll see you tomorrow."

"Can't wait."

Once the sedan had pulled away from the

curb, Griff tucked his girl close. "You gonna make it to the car, or do I need to carry you?"

"Mmm, last time you did that was our honeymoon."

Well, that just set off a kaleidoscope of erotic memories that were going to have to wait. She was way too tired tonight.

He scooped her up, cuddling her against his chest. "You were a beautiful bride."

"Mmm. Missed out on the white dress routine. But damn, you looked good in that suit."

He filed that away as something else to investigate. Right now, he needed to get her to bed.

CHAPTER 14

J ill lasted all of five steps out of the hotel lobby. "Oh. My. God. Now that we're alone, you have to tell me everything. You and Griff Powell? That is nerd girl dreams coming true. Dish!"

Sam groaned. "I need more coffee for that discussion." She'd missed out on the chance for it before leaving the hotel because Griff had other notions about the best way to wake up. She definitely hadn't argued with him about staying in bed. Or the shower. But it meant she'd been rushed when it came time to meet her friend.

"You have the look of a woman who's been well satisfied." Jill looped an arm through Sam's. "I'd hate you for that on principle, but I know how far back your feelings for him go, so I'll restrain myself in exchange for details."

"I'm not giving you a blow by blow of my love life."

"That's fine. I'm really more interested in what he's done for you."

Sam's face caught fire. "Jill!"

Unabashed, she only shrugged. "What? You can't expect me not to be curious. The man is even hotter now than he was in high school. We always speculated about whether his performance lived up to the package. So to speak."

"He's certainly exceeded my expectations. And they weren't low."

Jill's delighted cackle had heads turning. "I'm plying you with coffee and pastries to get more out of you."

"You can try."

But Jill hadn't been her best friend since

fifth grade for nothing. The chocolate crois-
sants had Sam folding like a cheap card table.
By the end of their very late breakfast and
second round of coffee, Jill was fanning herself.

"Girl. That is just... whew. So what is this,
really? You said last night y'all were starting
over. Is this a flaming hot affair or are you really thinking about forever with him?"

"Yes?" Sam couldn't stop the tone of uncer-
tainty in her own voice. Hadn't she been asking
herself this same question?

"To which?"

"To both. This all got started again because
the chemistry is undeniably still there. And I
believe he truly regrets how things ended before. He says he still wants the whole kit and
caboodle. Marriage. Kids. Forever."

"But do you?"

"That depends on who you're asking. If
you're asking your very down-to-earth, practical friend of twenty years, she'd say that we'll
see. That it takes time to rebuild trust, and it's
only sensible to take our time to build the foun-

dation we didn't have before. But that's not who I am when I'm with him. I'm still that deliriously in-love girl who said yes when he said he wanted forever the first time."

"Even though he left?"

"Even though. I don't believe he'd do it again. He has so many regrets about hurting me, and he's not the same guy who thinks he has to earn me."

"So where does that leave you?"

That was the million dollar question.

"Torn between the urge to be sensible and the desire to take that reckless leap again, because a part of me is still afraid I'll wake up alone. That part wants to hang on and not let go, even though there are eleven thousand details about merging our real lives together that we should discuss first."

Jill slouched in her chair, considering. "I mean, we are in Vegas. You could ask him this time."

Sam stared at her. "Just up and propose to him."

"Why not? This is the twenty-first century. We aren't bound by the same social rules we used to be. You want to marry him, and you're in the marriage capital of the world. Again."

She had a point. And yet... "I'm enough of a traditionalist that I still want to be the one asked. Actually, he didn't exactly ask the first time. He blurted out that we should get married."

"So it was impulse rather than a formal, romantic, down-on-one knee scenario? Still seems like you were swept off your feet."

"Oh, I was."

"What else do you wish you'd done differently before? Worn gold lame? Had Elvis officiate?"

"None of that. Our wedding was small but sweet. The only thing really missing was family and friends. But in the end, that was a good thing. I don't know what Jonah would have done if he'd been there."

"Fair point."

"And then there was the dress."

"The dress?"

"I got married in my bridesmaid's dress from Chloe's wedding. I didn't care that much at the time, but if I'm going to do this again, I want to do it right."

Jill clapped her hands in glee. "I have an idea. We should go wedding dress shopping."

Sam arched a brow. "For the wedding I don't know I'm having? That seems like bad luck."

"It seems like fun. You don't have to actually buy anything. But then you'll know maybe more about what you like. It will save time down the line. Plus, a lot of bridal shops offer champagne with fittings. That seems like a win-win to me."

It was foolish. Presumptive. And, damn it, it sounded like fun.

"Let's do it."

Twenty minutes later, they were ensconced in a private alcove of the nearest bridal shop, with mimosas and an enthusiastic sales associate hauling out dresses of every shape and style. The sight of them had Sam's belly fluttering. She really shouldn't be doing this. It was putting the cart before the horse. But someone was shoving a strapless bra into her hand and nudging her behind a curtain with an ocean of tulle, organza, and silk.

From the other side, Jill called out. "Hang on, hang on. I've got you." A moment later, the unmistakable beginning of the Space Jams theme song rang out from her freshly charged phone, demanding, "Y'all ready for this?"

Sam doubled over with giggles and reached for the nearest hanger.

Jill pronounced the first dress, with its full princess skirt, "Too floofy." The second, a halter-top, A-line number with no ornamentation, was declared, "Too plain." The third, a mermaid-cut gown with an ivory lace overlay, made Sam feel like she was wearing a full body straight jacket.

She got into things with the fourth dress, even though the cathedral-length train weighed like forty pounds. She tried sequins and sashes and satins. By the start of her third mimosa, she was starting to lose energy and faith. This had been fun, but of course she wasn't going to find a dress today. She didn't even know she was having a wedding.

"Just one more," Jill insisted, hugging one to her chest.

"Fine. But after this, we really need to get back to our errands."

Sam carried the dress into the fitting room and stepped into it, grateful for the clerk's help in lacing up the corset-style bodice. The skirts were full but not ridiculous, and the subtle white-on-white embroidered pattern was elegant and romantic.

"Okay, keep your eyes closed," she ordered.

Sam did as ordered, stepping up onto the little dais in front of the wraparound mirror and waiting as they both fussed with the skirt and the draping of the dress.

"Oh, damn." At Jill's soft, reverent voice, she opened her eyes.

"Oh." Sam couldn't stop herself from

reaching out toward the reflection in the mirror. The strapless bodice had a sweetheart neckline. The corseting showed off her tiny waist and the skirts made her feel like she should be attending a ball. "It's beautiful."

"You're beautiful. That is The Dress. You need a tiara for your hair."

She could see it. Her long hair all done up in one of the fancy up-dos her mom specialized in, with a glittering princess tiara perched on top and dangling chandelier earrings. She'd never been a particularly girly girl, but this... this was the stuff dreams were spun from.

And she'd spent enough time dreaming today.

"It won't do me much good until I've secured the groom."

"You can fix that," Jill insisted. "Griff wants to marry you. He said so himself. So ask him first."

"More and more women are doing it," the clerk confirmed. "It's pretty cool seeing the patriarchy upset like that."

"I don't know."

In this, she was old-fashioned. She wanted the grand gesture of a romantic proposal. But maybe that didn't matter. At the end of the day, she just wanted Griff.

"Take the time to think about it. The dress will still be here tomorrow." Jill looked at the sales associate. "Y'all can hold it for a day or two?"

"Of course."

"Then you'll have time to make up your mind before y'all leave at the end of the week."

Her mind spun as she got out of the dress and back into her own clothes. Was she really going to think about proposing to Griff? After mere days of being back together? Why did that part matter? If he asked her, she'd say yes. She wanted him. Wanted the life they'd missed. And, damn, she really wanted this dress. So maybe. Maybe if he didn't do it first, she'd pull the trigger herself before they flew home. Then she could pick up the dress for… whenever their wedding actually ended up being.

Heart hammering with resolve, she stepped out of the dressing room. One way or another, she was leaving Vegas engaged.

* * *

"It's still beautiful," Sam murmured, looking out at the brightly lit Vegas skyline from their position near the top of the High Roller.

Griff didn't give a damn about any view but the woman he caged in against the rail. She'd been pensive since she got back from her outing. If not for Jill's enthusiastic thumbs up behind Sam's back at dinner, he might have been worried she was rethinking everything. But Sam had said the trip was bringing up a lot of stuff, and she didn't know how she'd feel about being here again.

He dropped a kiss to the juncture of her neck and shoulder, resisting the urge to linger and nuzzle. "Not the tallest Ferris wheel anymore. I think they built an even bigger one in Dubai."

"Mmm." She leaned back into him, relaxing on a sigh as his arms came around her.

"You okay?"

"Just tired. The last several days are catching up with me. There's been a lot of travel and not a lot of sleep."

That was in his favor. He needed her to sleep like the dead tonight, so she wouldn't notice when he slipped out to put the finishing touches on his surprise.

"Do you want to head back to the hotel? We don't have to do this walk down memory lane tonight." *Please say no.*

He'd gotten a hell of a lot done today, but there were still some final pieces to get into place. Thank God this city never really shut down.

She pivoted and looped her arms around his neck. "That seems a shame. We're only here a few more days. I can sleep when I get home."

"In that case, how about we hit up the Eiffel Tower next?"

"That is the correct order of things," she confirmed.

They had drinks at the bar on the observation deck, toasting their good fortune in finding each other again, as they had eight years ago. But Griff didn't miss her restlessness. She seemed somehow hyper-focused and distracted.

Wanting to bring her back from wherever her brain had gone, he laced his fingers with hers. "I'll never forget when we were here before."

Her attention returned to him with a warm smile. "It was a memorable trip."

"You were so excited about our little world tour right here in Vegas."

She laughed. "Small-town girl gets excited about the little things."

"You were adorable. Did you ever do any of that international travel? See any of the world like we talked about?"

"Not as much as I'd like. I did squeeze in a trip to the UK at the end of grad school. But mostly I've been on the publish or perish train of academia. I'm kind of a workaholic."

He had no trouble believing that. Her capacity to focus and lose herself in work had always astounded him. "Is that because you love what you do, or to keep yourself from thinking about other things?"

"Probably some of both," she conceded.

Griff brought her hand to his lips. "We should go."

"Where?"

"Anywhere you want. I like traveling with you, Professor. I like seeing how you look at the world. So we should plan a trip for after the wedding."

"The wedding?" she squeaked, her eyes going wide.

"You know. That thing we're standing up in for Kendrick and Erin in a few weeks?"

"Oh. Right." She looked away, color rising in her cheeks.

The truth struck him hard and fast.

She was waiting for him to propose again.

The realization almost had him leaping up to do a fist pump. A part of him had been concerned it was too soon, that she'd want to take their time and be absolutely certain. But she wanted this as much as he did. He thought about blowing half his plans and giving her exactly what she wanted. The ring was in his pocket. He could drop down right here and ask her. But he'd put so much into tomorrow, and when they looked back on this trip, he wanted her to have the whole big grand gesture. She deserved that kind of romance. So he'd wait until tomorrow, as he'd planned.

They kept up conversation about possible trip destinations as they made their way to the Venetian for the gondola ride that would wrap their evening. She was all but vibrating as he handed her into the boat. Of course she was. This was where he'd proposed the first time, blurting it out as the biggest, best way to commemorate their weekend. This go-round, he wanted her to know it wasn't an impulse, so he bit back the words that wanted to spill out, as their gondolier shoved off and began to sing, some full-bodied opera tune that echoed off the extraordinary ceiling that mimicked the sky.

"It's nice to be able to listen to Puccini again without being sad," she murmured.

"You like opera?"

"It's actually one of my favorite things to write to. Or used to be. I don't speak Italian, so I don't get distracted by the words. But I love all the emotion packed into the music."

"Just when I thought I knew everything about you."

Those gorgeous lips quirked. "I expect there's a lot you don't know yet."

He toyed with her hair, tucking it back from her face. "Plenty of time to learn. I'm not going anywhere."

Her throat worked, her eyes searching his face. "Griffin."

He smiled. She was almost the only one who used his full name. "Samantha."

She straightened, gripping his hands with hers and taking a breath. "Will you—"

The gondola lurched, the singing breaking off with a shout and a curse.

Griff kept his balance low, lest the rocking boat tip over. "What the hell?"

"Sorry! Sorry!" The gondolier from the boat that had apparently rammed theirs shouted an apology. "I'm new. I'm so sorry!"

In the flurry of more apologies from their gondolier, the whole mood of intimacy and secrets was lost. It wasn't until they were back at the dock that Griff remembered her question.

"What were you going to ask me?"

Color bloomed in her cheeks again as she looked with regret at the canal. "Nothing."

Oh hell. Had she been about to propose to *him*? He felt almost bad for the interruption. Almost. As flattering as it would be to be asked, he didn't want anything to ruin his grand gesture. He'd make up for the disappointment in spades. She'd see.

Just one more day.

CHAPTER 15

The room was still dark when Sam woke. For a long moment, she lay there in that foggy space before her brain came online, debating whether it was worth getting up or if she'd slide back into dreams. It took a minute to work up the energy to move, but when she did, the full-body stretch felt glorious, all her muscles yawning, her body popping back into proper alignment after a long, deep sleep. She felt well-rested for the first time in ages.

A glance at the bedside clock had her frowning. After ten. Which meant it wasn't early. It was late.

She rolled over to find an empty bed and light leaking in around the edges of the blackout contains.

"Griff?"

But the utter stillness of the room was her only answer. He wasn't here.

Ignoring the instinctive sinking in her stomach, she threw back the covers and switched on a light. The bathroom door was open. Definitely no Griff.

It was fine. This wasn't like eight years ago. He always woke with the sun. lying around while she slept the day away wasn't in his wheelhouse. He probably just got restless and went for a run, or wanted breakfast and didn't want to wake her. She'd been talking about being tired last night. He was just being considerate. She did feel better after logging more than ten hours of sleep.

"He'll be back by the time I finish my shower."

Satisfied with her own logic, she headed into the bathroom and indulged in a long, steaming shower, letting the hot water beat on all her muscles, especially the ones that had been getting a hell of a workout since she'd taken Griff back into her bed. Because she could, she scrubbed and buffed and shaved every inch. Then she smoothed on some of the luxe moisturizer that had come with the room. She definitely wanted some more of that to take home.

Slipping on the hotel bathrobe, she padded back into the bedroom. Still no Griff.

Biting her lip, she crossed to her phone. No text message of explanation. Not that he was much of a texter. She'd seen the appallingly ancient flip phone he used.

It was fine. He was picking up lunch. Or stuck in traffic. Or... something. She'd just call him.

But the call went straight to voicemail. "This is Griff. You know what to do."

"Hey, it's me. Sorry I slept half the day away. But I'm up now and raring to go on whatever adventure you've thought up. Call me when you get this."

Determined not to give in to the skitter of panic and dread, she got dressed and dried her hair, keeping an eye on her phone the whole time.

But he didn't call. He didn't text.

She tried calling him again, still with no answer.

Refusing to just sit and freak out, she decided to channel her anxiety into productivity. She'd scattered her things all over the room. She'd pick up and organize, make life easier for housekeeping.

Hands shaking, she began gathering up dirty clothes, neatly folding and packing them back in her suitcase. Griff was so much neater. Probably a holdover from the Marines. None of his stuff was on the floor.

Her hands stilled on a sweater. She hadn't seen any of his stuff in the bathroom, either.

With a mounting sense of doom, she put the sweater aside and slowly moved to check. But his dop kit was gone. No toothbrush sat beside hers, no beard trimmer was plugged into the wall.

It didn't mean anything. He'd just picked up while she was sleeping to give himself something to do.

Even though they weren't leaving for two more days.

Heart pounding, she opened the closet door. But his duffel wasn't on the floor. It wasn't jammed up on the shelf. And when she tore through the rest of the room with frenetic desperation, it wasn't anywhere else either. There was no sign anywhere that he'd been here at all.

Griff was gone.

And this time there was no note. No half-assed explanation. Nothing. Because there was nothing formal to dissolve. They weren't still married. He hadn't given in to all the nostalgia of being here again and asked her. He hadn't even touched her last night, saying she needed the sleep.

Had he already been putting distance between them?

Nausea roiled in her belly.

God, she'd been a fool. She'd fallen under his spell again. Given him her heart, her body, her trust. And he'd left her.

Again.

Betrayal sliced through her like a jagged knife, ripping open the heart that had only just healed, and leaving her bloody and aching.

Unable to hold back the storm of emotion beating to get out, she collapsed on the bed. Tears ran scalding down her cheeks as her breath tore out in ragged sobs.

How could she have been so stupid? How could she have been so wrong? She'd have bet her life that he loved her, that he regretted leaving the first time. She'd bet her heart that he'd never do it again. She'd been so certain she'd tried on *wedding dresses,* for God's sake.

Her calculated risk had turned out to be a bad bet, and she'd lost everything that mattered.

She cried hard and long, until her head throbbed and there wasn't a drop of moisture left in her body. Then she lay in a shuddering heap on the bed, wishing she'd never laid eyes on Griff Powell again.

When the hard knock sounded on the door, she couldn't even muster the energy to tell housekeeping to go away. They'd figure it out soon enough, when they came inside. But when the knock came again, she dragged herself out of bed and crossed the room, pulling open the door.

But it wasn't housekeeping.

It was her brother, looking larger than life, his big frame filling the doorway. The dark hair that had grown out since his surgery was rumpled, as were his clothes. He had a duffel bag over one shoulder and what counted as a cheerful smile on his face.

For a long moment she could only stare,

watching as his expression shifted to concern, then anger.

"Jonah, what are you doing here?" Her ravaged throat croaked the words.

"Well, I came to walk you down the aisle, but given current circumstances, I'm happy to kick his ass instead."

And on that pronouncement, he shoved inside.

* * *

AFTER TWELVE YEARS in the Marines, Griff had thought he knew what FUBAR meant.

He'd been wrong.

His carefully crafted surprise had gone entirely sideways, and he hadn't made it back to the hotel. There wasn't a chance in hell Sam wasn't awake by now. God knew what she thought. He'd worked so hard to allay her fears over the past week, but with no explanation for his absence, what else *could* she think but the absolute worst? And now he was stuck in traffic because an eighteen-wheeler had collided with a poultry truck and chickens were running all over the street, while emergency personnel tried to deal with the resulting snarl of traffic.

He laid on his horn, needing to do something. "Come on!"

"I don't think that's going to help."

Griff glared at Jill in the passenger seat. "At this rate, it'll take an hour to get two miles. I don't have an hour."

"How fast is your mile?"

"What?"

"You know what? Doesn't matter. It's guaranteed faster than this." She released her seatbelt. "In the time-honored tradition of panicked romance movie heroes everywhere, you're gonna make a run for it."

He looked at the bags in the backseat. "What about—"

"I'll bring everything. None of it's going to do a damned bit of good if you lose the girl. Go."

He couldn't lose Sam. Not after this. More people honked as he slid out of the driver's side.

Jill raced around the front of the car and slid behind the wheel. "Good luck! I'll be behind you as soon as I can."

Griff took off, dodging between cars and around trucks until he was running flat out, thanking God for all his years of physical conditioning. He skirted the accident, shooting out the other side so fast that he caught a rogue chicken with his foot and sent it flying with a squawk. He faltered, watching it flap its wings and crash down onto the hood of a minivan. A sedan clipped him in the process, hard enough to spin him around, but he was already running again when the driver called out, "Hey buddy, are you okay?"

He wasn't. Wouldn't be until he set things right with Sam.

Please let her still be here.

Pedestrians and drivers alike stared as he flew by. Sweat poured down his back, and his muscles burned as he ate up the distance. Still, he dug for more speed as he caught sight of the hotel. At a dead run, he sprinted across the circular drive, right into the path of an oncoming car. Unable to stop, he put out a hand and launched himself over the hood, hitting the pavement running on the other side, even as tires screeched. The automatic doors opened to the lobby, and he made a beeline across the marble floor, leaping over bags and planters, dodging other guests. People were shouting, but he didn't slow. Not wanting to wait for the elevator, he hit the fire stairs, bolting up three at a time. From somewhere below, he heard pounding footsteps. Probably security.

He'd explain himself later.

By the time he made it to the eighth floor, his breath was wheezing and his legs were screaming. Dragging his key card out on the run, he was ready when he reached their room, slamming it into the lock and falling through the door on a gasp. "Samantha, I—"

His words were cut off as someone slammed him into a wall. Adrenaline spiking, he barely stopped himself from defensive countermeasures as he registered a furious Jonah Ferguson gripping the front of his shirt.

"You made my sister cry. Give me one good reason I shouldn't break you."

"Jonah!" Sam's voice had Griff's legs giving out.

She was still here.

"Let him go!"

On a growl, Jonah reluctantly did as ordered, and Griff slid down the wall. He was shaking, unable to get his limbs to cooperate. Jesus, the adrenaline crash was hell. But he had to get to Sam, had to explain.

Then she was there, kneeling beside him, worry mingling with grief on her pretty face. His gut twisted as he took in her puffy, red-rimmed eyes. She'd thought the worst then.

Desperate, he reached for her hand. "I didn't leave. I swear to you. I'd never do that to you again."

"Again?" Jonah snarled.

Sam pulled her hand away, and fresh panic fluttered in his chest. "All your stuff is gone."

"Not gone. Moved. I was supposed to be back before you woke up, but everything went all to hell when I got arrested."

Her brows drew together, her mouth dropping open. "When you what now?"

This was all coming out wrong. "I wanted to surprise you. There was supposed to be a flash mob at the fountain at the Bellagio."

"I... what?"

"I thought you'd dig that for a proper proposal this time."

"This time?"

"Shut up, Jonah," she snapped. "I don't understand. Why would your stuff need to be moved for that?"

"It's in the honeymoon suite." It was all spilling out like so much word vomit now. "I had the wedding planned for this afternoon, with your brother and your mom flying in, so we did it right this time."

"You married my sister before?" Jonah demanded.

Another female voice hushed him.

Sam seemed to be struggling to follow his disjointed tale. "And the arrest?"

"It happened while Jill and I were out finalizing details." He sucked in another unsteady breath. "Some jack-off thought it was okay to grab her ass. I disabused him of that notion with my fist. He put up a bit of a fight—" Someone shoved a bottle of water into his hand. "Thanks." He paused to guzzle half of it. "By the time I put him down, the cops showed up. Turns out he's the son of some high-up muckity-muck with connections. Had me arrested on the spot. It took a while to go before the judge. The charges were dropped, but by then it was too late." Tipping up the bottle, he drained the last of it.

Sam rubbed at her temple. "Why didn't you call?"

"My phone broke in the fight, and Jill's apparently fell out of her purse somewhere along the way. We figured the best chance was to get back here to explain before you got on a plane, but there was a wreck blocking the road, so I ran the rest of the way. She's got the car."

Sam opened her mouth, then closed it again, clearly not sure what to say.

"I'm sorry. I'm so fucking sorry for worrying you. I know what you must have thought. I'd never deliberately put you through that." This time, when he reached out to cup her check, she didn't pull back. "I wanted to make a grand gesture, but I just fucked it all up."

Her eyes softened, and he knew he had to do this now. Without all the trappings he'd planned. Because his lungs were no longer heaving like a bellows, he rolled to one knee, pulling out the ring box. "This isn't the flash mob. It's not the romance you deserve, but in the name of absolute clarity, I love you. I've loved you for eight years. From the time you first walked down that aisle to me, through every burning desert, on every freezing mountain, during every miserable drill and deployment in between. I love you. And I hope I haven't ruined all chance of you agreeing to be my wife again. Will you marry me, Samantha? Today, next week, next year. At a time of your choosing? Because obviously I can't be trusted to plan anything. But you can trust me to love you, to twine my roots, my fate, with yours from this day forward."

Tears slid down her cheeks again. "You remembered."

"Every word." He'd give her back the vows she made to him all these years ago. "Say yes, Professor."

She swallowed. "There's something I need to know."

"Anything."

"Were you actually planning to dance and/or sing as part of the flash mob?" The corners of her mouth twitched, belying her sober expression.

"Well, no. They were more like background. I planned all this in about thirty-six hours. There wasn't time to learn choreography."

"Too bad. That'd have been something to see."

"If that's what it takes, I'll make it happen." He'd do anything to salvage this relationship. She was the most precious thing in his life, and he couldn't lose her to a stupid twist of fate and straight up bad luck.

Sam shook her head. "No. It's too late."

Griff's heart sank.

"I mean… the wedding's at two, and you're really gonna need a shower."

He stared. "What? You're saying yes?"

"Mom and Jonah told me what you had planned. Some of it anyway." Her smile bloomed. "It seems a shame to let it go to waste."

"Thank God." He slid the ring on her finger and hauled her into his arms, kissing her with all the love and relief that flooded through him.

The volume of cheers had him breaking away to finally look at the small crowd gathered in their room. In addition to Jonah and Rebecca, a red-headed woman stood grinning beside a familiar face he hadn't expected to see.

"Whitmore? What the hell are you doing here?"

Brax Whitmore saluted. "Master Sergeant. Turns out it's a small world. I'm in the same treatment program as Ferguson here. When he said he was coming out and mentioned your name, I knew you had to be the same Griff Powell who hauled my ass to safety after that firefight went all to hell. Figured I'd tag along so you had someone standing up for you."

"That's..." Griff swallowed, moved by the gesture from an entirely different kind of brother. "Thanks, man. I appreciate it."

"Least I can do after you saved my life."

Griff swung his attention to the redhead. "I'm guessing you're Audrey?"

She beamed. "I am. So nice to meet you."

Rebecca clapped her hands. "Okay, the meet and greet is over. You can visit after. We've only got an hour to get you both ready. So hop to it. Boys, out! Y'all follow Griff up to the other suite and get out of my way. I have beauty miracles to perform to fix the aftermath of that crying jag."

Smiling now, Sam stood, helping him to his feet. "Oh, but I have nothing to wear."

Just then, another knock sounded.

Griff crossed on wobbly legs and pulled it open.

Jill stepped inside, garment bags in her arms. "Did somebody order a wedding dress?"

CHAPTER 16

The moment the door shut behind the men, Sam sank down on the edge of the bed. Relief and joy mingled with exhaustion from the emotional roller coaster of the past few hours, leaving her legs and hands shaking. In just over an hour, she'd marry the man she loved. Again. And he'd made sure she'd have family and friends this time. The sweetness of the gesture, no matter how much of the plan got botched, had fresh tears welling.

"No ma'am. No more tears until after all this is over. Here, guzzle this." Rebecca thrust a bottle of water into her hands and began digging into the bag she'd brought with the tools of her trade.

Sam dutifully drank and tried to pull back all the emotion that wanted to burst out. "I'm really glad y'all are all here. It means a lot that you'd come all this way on such short notice."

"My only daughter's getting married. Wild horses couldn't have kept me away. Here, head back. These drops will fix the bloodshot."

Abruptly worried about her mother's no-nonsense reaction, Sam reached out to grasp her hand. "I'm sorry I didn't tell you about before. I never told anybody."

"Baby, I understand. I knew you were hurting something awful back then." She began smoothing some sort of cream over Sam's cheeks. "And frankly, it's a comfort to me it wasn't over that Eric boy you dated first year of grad school. Griff makes so much more sense."

Sam blinked. "He does?"

"Honey, I always knew you two had feelings for each other."

"You did?" How could Rebecca have known what Sam hadn't realized herself at the time?

"Of course. I saw how you both used to look at each other. You wore your heart on your sleeve, and Griff—well, he used to look at you like a kid, staring at the thing he wanted most in the world and never expected to have. And even if I hadn't seen all that, the little scene I walked in on in your old bedroom made it plenty clear."

"Oh God." Sam tried to hide her burning cheeks.

"I feel like you left out part of the story," Jill accused, dropping backward onto the straight-backed chair at the desk and folding her arms across the top. "What did you walk in on?"

Rebecca's green eyes twinkled with mirth. "Nature on the verge of taking its course. Before the clothes came off."

Jill hooted with laughter.

It was official. Sam was going to die of embarrassment before she ever made it down the aisle.

"Sorry about the timing, honey. Though I suspect y'all took care of that somewhere along this trip."

"Mom!"

"What? Good chemistry is important in a marriage. Though I don't think that was ever your problem."

"No." She heaved a sigh and opted to address the elephant in the room. "Look, I know this seems fast and maybe a little crazy. Especially in light of our previous marriage and divorce. But we weren't ready for each other before. We are now. And even though there are a ton of details we haven't worked out, I want you to know I've thought this through. I love him. I've always loved him. We'll figure out everything else as we go."

Rebecca framed Sam's face between her palms, staring down with so much love. "Sweetheart, I'm not worried. Even if we hadn't all been witness to that speech he gave when he got here, I knew he loved you when he called to get me here."

"What exactly did he say? He hadn't even proposed yet."

"Well, the specifics are between him and me, but the gist was that he'd been in love with you for years, and he'd worked to make himself into the kind of man you deserved, and that if you said yes, he'd spend the rest of his life adoring and taking care of you. A mother can't ask for anything more than that."

Sam waved both hands at her face. "Damn it. I'm trying not to cry again."

"Well, I'm guessing it'll be safe to say you will no longer hate weddings after today," Audrey hypothesized.

"No. No, I won't." She held out her hand, admiring the simple, princess-cut diamond solitaire he'd chosen for her.

Jill gave a satisfied sigh. "I can't wait to see you flash that ring in Cressida's face when we get back to Eden's Ridge for Kendrick and Erin's wedding. I promise I'll video the whole thing for posterity."

"As appealing an idea as that is, I don't want to make a big deal out of it."

"Seriously? After everything she's done to you?"

"It's not about taking the high road. It's Kendrick and Erin's wedding. I don't want to do anything to take away from their day. It was bad enough I got into it with Cressida during the bachelor/bachelorette weekend."

Eyebrows shot up around the room.

Audrey hummed her therapist's that's-interesting noise. "I feel like there's a story there."

"I'm going to regret missing that, aren't I?" Jill asked.

"If you hadn't, I don't know that we'd be here right now, so I'll say thank you from the bottom of my heart."

"Damn it. I'm gonna get all misty. Subject change! Let's talk hair. Mama Ferguson, how do you feel about tiaras?"

"Oh girl, you know I love a good tiara!"

"I grabbed one when I picked up the dress."

Sam eyed the garment bag. "Is that really The Dress?"

Jill's grin was smug and delighted. "Of course it is."

She shook her head. "You were in on his plan the whole time."

"Bet your ass. If anyone deserves a grand gesture, it's you. Sorry it got derailed."

Sam caught her hands and squeezed. "Thank you for helping give me a beautiful wedding."

"It's the least I can do since you both up-ended your lives for the last week in the name of finding me."

Rebecca nudged Jill out of the way and began fussing with Sam's hair. "Audrey, you're on bobby pin duty. Hold these."

"Yes, ma'am."

Sam reached up to cover her mom's hand with hers. "I know this wasn't what you prob-ably expected. Are you disappointed not to get to plan the big white wedding, with all the pomp and circumstance?"

"I'm getting to help you get ready and watch

you marry the man you love. That's plenty for me. And God bless the boy for saving us all the months of stress."

"Maybe you'll get to do the big wedding with Jonah," Audrey suggested.

Sam laughed. "I'm sorry. I thought you'd met my brother. Big, taciturn, mission-driven. If he's had a relationship with a woman that's lasted more than a month since high school, I don't know about it."

Audrey angled her head, a considering expression on her face. "You never know."

Sam recognized that look. "What do you know?"

She held up her hands. "I don't know anything. I just think he's going to finally be in a place emotionally where he's ready to think about a different kind of life. That's all I'm saying about it. You have to finish getting ready, because we have to hit up the courthouse for a marriage license on the way."

* * *

THE WEATHER WAS PERFECT, with the sky stretching in a wide river of uninterrupted blue above the venue gardens. Flowers of all types perfumed the air. Tasteful arrangements accented the corners of the pavilion where Griff stood in his tux, waiting for Sam to walk down the aisle. Because she'd said yes. Again. Despite all the chaos and the hurt, she'd said yes. The miracle of that had him all but bouncing in his dress shoes, and he was grateful there was no protracted waiting period, because he didn't think he could stand it. The cancellation he'd stumbled on at this full-service venue, during the course of his planning, had been a gift from the Universe. One he'd taken as a sign that this was meant, here and now.

He chuckled to himself, thinking Sam's romanticism was rubbing off on him. He wouldn't have it any other way.

Beside him, Brax fidgeted, tugging at the cuffs of his tux shirt and twitching his broad shoulders.

"Man, what's up with you? You're acting like you're the groom."

On a short laugh, Brax shook his head. "It just feels weird being up here in a monkey suit."

Griff remembered him saying that his own wedding had been a courthouse affair. No fancy duds. No friends and family. "Well, for what it's worth, looks good on you. I appreciate you being willing to do this."

"Happy to. I'm glad it worked out for you, man. I know how much you wanted this."

"You never know. It could work out for you, too, if you just reach out to find her. Hell, the internet's an amazing thing. Sam's a whiz at tracking down information. I'm sure she'd be happy to help try to find her."

Brax just shook his head. "It's not the same thing. I wasn't the one who left."

Which didn't matter a damn, because Griff was well aware the man was still in love with his ex-wife. It was something they'd bonded over during their time in the service.

"If that were true, this wouldn't still be stuck

in your craw." Remembering what Sam had said at the bonfire, he turned toward his friend. "Closure's worth a hell of a lot. Either way, you need answers."

The start of the music cut off any reply Brax might have made. He turned resolutely toward the head of the aisle, bearing straight and tall, like the Marine he'd been. Letting it go, Griff faced the start of the long white runner himself. Then he saw Sam and everything else fell out of his head.

She was radiant, her long glossy brown hair bundled up in a mass of fancy twists and curls, crowned by an honest-to-God, sparkly tiara. But the bling she wore was nothing to her smile as she began walking down that aisle on her brother's arm. He remembered seeing her walking down the aisle the first time. He'd wanted her. He'd loved her. And he'd thought he was the luckiest bastard on earth. But he hadn't felt the bone-deep certainty of forever. Not like he did now. This time, she wasn't the only one who believed he was worthy.

They reached the pavilion, and the officiant began.

"Dearly beloved, we are gathered here today to join Griffin and Samantha in holy matrimony. Who gives this woman to be wed?"

"Her mother and I," Jonah replied.

He transferred her hand to Griff's and gave him a long, narrow look. "Take care of her." The *I'm coming after you if you don't* was implied.

But Griff wasn't worried. This was it. The real deal.

He helped her up the one step to the altar, and they both followed the officiant's directions, until it came time to give their vows.

Griff sucked in a breath and let it out slowly, feeling himself settle as he looked into her beautiful brown eyes and slid the ring onto her finger. "The last time we did this, I gave you someone else's words. Today, I'm sticking with mine. We've known each other a long, long time, and over the years, we've been a lot of things to each other. Through all of it, you've been this miraculous, quiet support. I'm an incredibly lucky man to have had you in my corner, believing in me the way you do. You've made me a better man, and as I make these vows to you, know that I mean them for always, 'for it was not into my ear you whispered, but into my heart.' I've carried you here for eight years," He tapped his chest over the tattoo that had been a constant reminder of what he strove for. "And for the rest of our days, I swear to love, honor, and cherish you, to continue to do the work to deserve you for the rest of our lives, and I promise never to try to surprise you again."

She laughed and squeezed his hands, and Griff thought his heart would burst from the joy of it. Nothing on earth would ever be better than her smile as she slid the ring on his finger.

"You're absolutely right. We've known each other a long time, and we've been through a lot together. I loved you through your wild days, through your hard days, and through all the days you were away from me, trying to find yourself. And I'm going to love you through all our future days together. I swear to love, honor, and cherish you, to trust you, to see you, and to encourage you, for 'it was not my lips you kissed, but my soul.' It's yours and ever will be."

Tears burned the backs of his eyes, and he was man enough not to blink them away. She was his greatest gift, and today was the best day of his life.

"Griffin and Samantha, having proclaimed your love and commitment to each other in the eyes of these loved ones, and by the power vested in me by the state of Nevada, I now pronounce you husband and wife. You may kiss the bride."

Griff pulled her in, laying his lips over hers and dipping her back to the enthusiastic cheering of their small group of friends and family. She was his wife. His *wife.* At last, the part of his world that had been out of kilter for years snapped back into place. He was never letting her go again.

Sam was breathless and laughing by the time he righted her. Her hands skimmed over his shoulders to link behind his neck, pulling him down until his brow touched hers. "We did it."

"Damned straight. I love you, Samantha."

"Love you back, Griffin. Ever and always."

"Uh, hey, guys? There's the recessional, still."

Griff lifted his head to find that the world had not, in fact, disappeared, and the song was more than halfway over. With a sheepish grin, they untangled, and he escorted his bride back down the aisle to begin the next phase of their life. With cake.

EPILOGUE

"You know, I thought the ceremony was beautiful, but this reception —" Sam looked around the high-ceilinged space, festooned with twinkle lights and autumnal floral arrangements. "I never would have imagined the old mill could look like this."

"Porter and his crew did a hell of a job converting it into the Artisan Guild, but it was his wife Maggie's idea to lease it out for events," Abbey Keenan explained.

A band was setting up on the little raised stage, and a dance floor had been set up in the center. A buffet of Athena's mouth-watering creations took up almost all of the opposite wall. All around the edges of the massive room were tables for the many guests, which included a multitude of former fosters of Joan Reynolds and several of Kendrick's and Erin's students and colleagues from the high school. The love and celebration in the room was palpable.

"I'm surprised she's got time to do that. Erin told me a few weeks ago that Maggie was heading up that new small-business incubator."

"She is. They're looking for a new general manager for the Guild and maker's space."

"Sweets for my sweet." Abbey's husband, Kyle, swept in with a plate of wedding cake.

Beaming, Abbey rubbed the mound of her very pregnant belly. "Hank thanks you."

Griff slid into the next chair with two more slices of cake. "Did he seriously talk you into naming the kid after Hank Williams?"

Abbey laughed. "No, the baby's been dubbed Hank because he's made me as big as a tank. If he goes full term, I'll be giving birth to a Butter-ball turkey."

Sam felt a pinch of yearning as Kyle bent to kiss the baby belly. "Turkey was always my favorite."

Abbey skimmed a hand through Kyle's blonde hair in an easy gesture of adoration. "Yeah, well, the little freeloader needs to hurry on up! I want my body back."

Kyle shifted to kiss her cheek. "Six more weeks."

Abbey groaned. "That's forever! At least I'll have my cousin to distract me this week. She gets here tomorrow."

At the mention of Abbey's cousin, Sam straightened, exchanging a look with Griff.

"Which cousin?" he asked.

Abbey forked up cake. "Given how many I have, that's a reasonable question. Livia. She's part of the Mississippi branch of the family. I think you met her forever ago that summer you worked at the orchard."

Ah ha. So Declan's infamous first love would be back in town for the first time in who knew how long. Wasn't that interesting?

Aiming for casual, Sam dug into her own cake. "That'll be nice. How long will she be in town?"

"A couple weeks. Her side of the family runs a Christmas tree farm, so this is her last chance to get away before their busy season." Abbey scraped the last of the icing from the plate and made sad eyes. "This cake is so good. I may need another piece."

"Well, you are eating for two. Growing a human takes a lot of calories! C'mon. We'll take a lap around the room for you to decide if there's really enough room in there with Hank the Tank tap dancing on your organs." Kyle hefted his wife to her feet. "See y'all later."

As they walked away, Griff scooted his chair closer, slipping an arm around Sam's shoulders.

She tipped her head to his. "Are you thinking what I'm thinking?"

Gooseflesh rose in the wake of the fingers he danced lightly down the outside of her arm as he turned to murmur in her ear, "That we sneak away from this reception and find a private spot for another attempt at making one of those ourselves?"

Sam sucked in a breath and dropped her hand to his thigh, where it was very obvious her husband was more than ready to pick up where they'd left off last night. She rubbed her thighs together in a vain attempt to assuage the ache. "I was actually thinking we should let Declan know he finally has a shot at talking to Livia again, but he can wait. I like your idea much better."

Griff tugged her up, sliding an arm around her waist and positioning her in front of him to camouflage the bulge in his tux pants. "C'mon."

"Think anyone will miss us?"

"I'm positive I don't care." He steered her toward the edge of the space, out of the glow from the twinkle lights.

Abbey had said there were classrooms on

the other floors. Surely one of them would be empty and have a lock...

Ari Bohannon popped into their path. "Where are y'all off to? It's time for the garter and bouquet toss! I've been tasked with rounding everyone up."

Griff growled low in his throat, his fingers flexing on Sam's hip.

"Sure, we'll be right there," she promised.

When Ari only stared at them with the expectant face of a kindergarten teacher herding recalcitrant children, they reluctantly headed back to the festivities.

Sam tipped her mouth up to Griff's ear. "Later."

He nipped her lobe in response, and she shuddered.

From the stage, the emcee for the night called out, "Alright, alright! Let's have all the single men down here on the floor for the garter toss!"

Several guys headed to the space in front of the stage. Griff didn't move an inch.

Kendrick spotted him and made a come-on gesture. "My man! You should be out here."

Griff just shook his head, hands in his pockets, shoulders square and solid, an immovable rock.

The crowd continued to urge him, "Come on, Griff!"

"Take the shot!"

"Don't be a party pooper!"

Ari folded her arms, brows arched high. "Is there some *reason* you don't want to participate?"

Oh hell, the kid knew. Sam had no idea how, but there was no mistaking the twinkle in her eye.

At Griff's inhale, she met his gaze and angled her head in question.

Should we?

He tilted his head in response. *Your call.*

Ari watched the exchange and crowed. "The jig is up! Spill, you two!"

Blood heated Sam's cheeks as all focus turned to them. This wasn't at all what she'd wanted.

Griff pointed at the girl. "Menace." But there was no heat to it.

He looked back at Sam. They'd discussed this in advance, and he'd agreed that they shouldn't take the focus off Kendrick and Erin. But they were making a bigger spectacle by not answering, so she nodded. He passed her the rings he'd been carrying in his pocket all day, and they both held up their left hands.

It seemed everyone in the room lost their collective minds. The roar was immense.

"You're married!"

"When did this happen?"

"Holy crap!"

"This is amazing!"

"Called it!" Ari shouted.

Kendrick let out a two-finger whistle and everybody quieted down. "I think I speak for everybody when I say, how long you been keeping this under your hat?"

"We didn't want to do anything to overshadow your day," Sam explained.

Erin waved that away. "Screw that! You got married! I knew you two would be great together, but I never expected this."

Griff shrugged. "We just got back from Vegas a couple weeks ago."

Kendrick stomped his feet in apparent delight, covering a grin with his fist. "You got married in Vegas again!"

"Again?" Erin exclaimed. "You mean that whole never have I ever thing, you married each other?"

Sam offered a sheepish smile. "Yeah."

"You evil, evil secret keeper!" Erin danced over and threw her arms around them both. "This is so awesome!" Then she turned back to her husband. "Wait, you knew about this, and you didn't tell me?"

"Babe, I was sworn to secrecy at the highest level. We all were."

Sam arched a brow at Griff. "Did you tell all of them?"

"Well, we figured it out during the bachelor party," Declan explained. "But thank God it's out now. I thought I was gonna explode wanting to talk about it."

Mick gave him a fist bump. "Word."

Past his shoulder, Sam caught sight of Cressida on the sidelines, looking like she'd been poleaxed. Her expression twisted, as if she'd caught a whiff of dead skunk while sucking a lemon. As Sam watched, she turned to the nearest table and gripped the edge.

Before she could shout out a warning, Cressida let out a banshee cry and straight up flipped the table. Dishes crashed and shattered, guests scattered, some screaming, plenty staring in absolute shock. Under the startled scrutiny of the entire reception, Cressida's cheeks flushed beet red and she spun, bolting for the nearest exit.

In the ensuing silence, Erin kept her arm around Sam's shoulders. "Well, I wanted her to show her ass bad enough Mom would stop guilting me about her. I'd say mission accomplished. Thanks for that bonus wedding present."

Jill sidled up. "Got the whole thing on my phone. Told you her reaction would be gold."

If Cressida had cried or seemed human in any way, Sam might've felt a little bad, but in the face of that tantrum, she couldn't quite muster it up.

As conversation returned to a buzz around them, Sam winced. "Look, we didn't want to make a big deal about this. Partly because of—well, that—but mostly because it's your wedding day. The focus should be on you."

"Hell no. This just became a couples' party," Kendrick declared.

And because the bride and groom deemed it so, everybody fell in line.

Toasts and well wishes were offered all around, and Erin and Kendrick insisted they get their own first dance.

As they circled the floor to Ed Sheeran's

"Thinking Out Loud," Griff smiled down at Sam. "Well, we did miss this part of the process. No big party the way we did it."

She pressed closer, smiling up at him. "Our wedding was absolutely perfect for us. I didn't miss a thing. I got you. At the end of the day, that's all I really wanted."

He bent his head to kiss her. "I love you."

Cameras flashed around them. Smiling, Sam shook her head. "I guess we made a bit of a splash with our unplanned announcement."

"I blame Ari. That kid has some kind of bloodhound nose about romance."

"Eh, one of these days she'll get her comeuppance when her mom and aunts get in on being nosy about her love life. And at least we don't have to hide it anymore. I like everybody knowing you're mine."

"If there's anybody in the county who doesn't know yet, they will by morning. The brain and the brawler got hitched."

Sam beamed up at him. "And they're going to live happily ever after."

GET YOUR BONUS CONTENT!

For once, I actually have another bonus epilogue because I *adore* Griff and Sam and there was another glimpse of their happily ever after I wanted to show. Get your copy here!

And in case you started here and want to go back to read Sam and Griff's beginning during that infamous weekend in Vegas, be sure to grab your copy of *Until We Meet Again.*

CHOOSE YOUR NEXT ROMANCE!

IF YOU'RE into sexy summer camp flings, you will definitely want to go back and check out Audrey's romance with her personal hero firefighter Hudson in my RITA® Award-Winning novel, *Second Chance Summer.* Their story will always hold a special place in my heart.

Or maybe you've got a yen for more second chance romance? Have you started the original Misfit Inn series? It begins with the second chance homecoming of Kennedy Reynolds and it's the book that started the Eden's Ridge Universe. Grab your copy of *When You Got A Good Thing* today!

OTHER BOOKS BY KAIT NOLAN

A complete and up-to-date list of all my books can be found at https://kaitnolan.com.

* * *

THE MISFIT INN SERIES
SMALL TOWN FAMILY ROMANCE

- *When You Got A Good Thing* (Kennedy and Xander)
- *Til There Was You* (Misty and Denver)
- *Those Sweet Words* (Pru and Flynn)

- *Stay A Little Longer* (Athena and Logan)
- *Bring It On Home* (Maggie and Porter)

RESCUE MY HEART SERIES
SMALL TOWN MILITARY ROMANCE

- *Baby It's Cold Outside* (Ivy and Harrison)
- *What I Like About You* (Laurel and Sebastian)
- *Bad Case of Loving You* (Paisley and Ty prequel)
- *Made For Loving You* (Paisley and Ty)

MEN OF THE MISFIT INN
SMALL TOWN SOUTHERN ROMANCE

- *Let It Be Me* (Emerson and Caleb)
- *Our Kind of Love* (Abbey and Kyle)
- *Don't You Wanna Stay* (Deanna and Wyatt)

- *Until We Meet Again* (Samantha and Griffin prequel)
- *Come A Little Closer* (Samantha and Griffin)

WISHFUL SERIES
SMALL TOWN SOUTHERN ROMANCE

- *Once Upon A Coffee* (Avery and Dillon)
- *To Get Me To You* (Cam and Norah)
- *Know Me Well* (Liam and Riley)
- *Be Careful, It's My Heart* (Brody and Tyler)
- *Just For This Moment* (Myles and Piper)
- *Wish I Might* (Reed and Cecily)
- *Turn My World Around* (Tucker and Corinne)
- *Dance Me A Dream* (Jace and Tara)
- *See You Again* (Trey and Sandy)
- *The Christmas Fountain* (Chad and Mary Alice)

- *You Were Meant For Me* (Mitch and Tess)
- *A Lot Like Christmas* (Ryan and Hannah)
- *Dancing Away With My Heart* (Zach and Lexi)

WISHING FOR A HERO SERIES (A WISHFUL SPINOFF SERIES)
SMALL TOWN ROMANTIC SUSPENSE

- *Make You Feel My Love* (Judd and Autumn)
- *Watch Over Me* (Nash and Rowan)
- *Can't Take My Eyes Off You* (Ethan and Miranda)
- *Burn For You* (Sean and Delaney)

MEET CUTE ROMANCE
SMALL TOWN SHORT ROMANCE

- *Once Upon A Snow Day*
- *Once Upon A New Year's Eve*

- *Once Upon An Heirloom*
- *Once Upon A Coffee*
- *Once Upon A Campfire*
- *Once Upon A Rescue*

SUMMER CAMP
CONTEMPORARY ROMANCE

- *Once Upon A Campfire*
- *Second Chance Summer*

ABOUT KAIT

Kait is a Mississippi native, who often swears like a sailor, calls everyone sugar, honey, or darlin', and can wield a bless your heart like a saber or a Snuggie, depending on requirements.

You can find more information on this RITA ®

Award-winning author and her books on her website http://kaitnolan.com.

Do you need more small town sass and spark? Sign up for her newsletter to hear about new releases, book deals, and exclusive content!

www.ingramcontent.com/pod-product-compliance
Lightning Source LLC
Chambersburg PA
CBHW060232100726
47907CB00003B/596